The Widow Smalls
and Other Stories

Jamie Lisa Forbes

Pronghorn Press
pronghornpress.org

For River, Dylan, Carter and Brody — this is how it was

The Stories

Ramona Dietz

The Widow Smalls and Other Stories

Snow flakes swirled around the barnyard, like one of those bubble toys, Roy mused, that you shake to watch the snow spin round. He stood transfixed in the sifting white, forgetting himself, forgetting his cattle. The drone of the truck engine bored into his skull at last—oh, his father would curse at the waste of gas—and he reached for the door handle, ready to climb in.

He felt a hand grasp his shoulder and he turned to see Norm, his hired hand. With Norm's snow goggles on, all Roy could make out were his jowls.

"Roy. I'm quitting."

"What?"

The truck rumbled. Snow rode the updrafts, fell again. Norm shuffled from foot to foot.

"I feel bad for ya. It's your dad. It's not you. I mean… He can call me a stupid sonofabitch if he likes, but to cuss out my wife…Roy, it ain't worth it."

This storm had drug Norm down—that was all.

"He doesn't mean half the crap he says. And he's only out here on weekends. We got the rest of the week to ourselves."

"We're leaving now."

"Now? We're weaning calves today. We're shipping 'em out next week!"

Norm sighed, as if he meant to feel guilty, but couldn't quite squeeze himself into it.

"Yeah, I know."

"We just ate breakfast!" Roy blasted, "Why didn't you tell me then?"

"I couldn't do it then, but when I came out here…" Norm looked up and snowflakes snagged in the ruff around his hood, "seems like I just don't want to do this anymore."

He stuck out his hand. Roy hesitated, then shook it, and although he meant to offer some words of thanks, his annoyance tongue-tied him and Norm disappeared around the corner of the barn without another word.

It was always something. Roy had been on the place for three years now, since 1955, and the one thing he'd learned was that ranching was no smooth business. If you squeezed enough water out of the snowmelt for hay, the hay machinery broke down. If you only lost one or two calves in the spring, the market dropped. If you had hay and a good calf crop and the market was strong and you were getting ready to wean and ship, the help quit.

He trudged toward his house. Well, the help always quit. Six months to a year was the best they'd kept 'em. Sometimes just two weeks. Sometimes just two days. Some of them, like Norman and Jeannie, were people his own age, people he liked. Most of them were just lazy drunks, as much of a burden as the cattle themselves.

As he slipped off his coveralls in the mudroom, he opened the door a crack. "Fran?" he called. He didn't want to startle her.

No answer. Just Ernest Tubb, faintly, on the radio. He walked through to the kitchen in his socks. Fran sat at their shiny chrome table, a cigarette smoldering between her fingers.

"Fran?" He leaned against the door frame.

"What are you doing home?" She turned to him, her eyes dark pools in her sallow face. With all the snow, she hadn't been outdoors in a month.

"Can you believe it? Norman quit!"

"Hmmm." Her gaze drifted back out to the snow. "Roy, do you think we could go out tonight?"

"Tonight? It's only Wednesday!"

"I haven't been to town all week."

"It's snowing, honey."

She drew the cigarette up and inhaled slowly. "It's always snowing."

It was hard these days to shove aside the nagging feeling that his wife was unhappy. Things had been so easy at first that he thought it was meant to be that way. He was the son of the town banker. She was the daughter of the town banker's lawyer. Everyone had said how perfect it was. And, of course, she'd follow him to the ranch.

He'd never ask her to work with him. She was above that, and besides, it was too hard for a woman. Every day he ate breakfast and lunch at the bunkhouse with the hired help so Fran wouldn't have to wake up early and cook. That left her alone, waiting for babies, among the plumped pieces of wedding furniture. But three years had gone by and no baby came.

He rang the bank, and when the secretary picked up, he turned away from Fran.

"Tully Carlton, please…Dad?"

"Yes." Tully's irritation at the interruption buzzed through the line.

"Norman quit."

"He'll stay for weaning today, won't he?"

Roy heard a click. They were on a party line with three other families. Since the listener wasn't hanging up, it had to be

Lillie Strader. He always struggled: what should he do, ignore her, or say "Ms. Lillie, if you don't mind, I'm using the phone." If he said anything, he'd break the flow of his own conversation and risk insulting her, which would be unwise the next time he needed her husband, Ollie, to come help brand.

He ignored her. "No. Norman says he's leaving now. I can't do it myself."

"We're shipping them out next week. Can't you get Ollie Strader to come help for today?"

Roy bit his thumbnail. "I don't know, Dad. I haven't talked to him."

"See if you can talk to him, or someone. I'll get some new help out as soon as I can."

Roy hung up the phone. Fran hadn't stirred. Cigarette smoke spiraled up from the ashtray. Lillie Strader was more interested in his weaning problem than Fran seemed to be.

The storm blew over during the night and the next morning billows of drifts sparkled in the rosy dawn. As the icy air filled his lungs, Roy didn't feel as bad as he had yesterday. Ollie said he'd come help after feeding and the snow wasn't too deep, so by the end of the day, the calves should be weaned. Come Sunday morning, they'd have a good brunch at the Country Club with Roy and Fran's parents, and it wouldn't be ruined by his father's displeasure at his failure to get the calves weaned.

He fed the hay by himself. The hush of winter dampened the crunch of hooves in the snow. Sunlight flooded the sky, and as he stood on the haystack and looked down, he thought how puny the operation was, even though his head was crammed full every day worrying about it.

His father's Cadillac was in the barnyard when he returned, along with a battered Dodge pickup. Roy followed the tracks to the bunkhouse. The sagging door was open—

he ought to fix that hinge, or get this new hand to fix it—and suitcases were stacked on the porch.

"Come in, son! I've brought you some new help."

Roy tried to knock his manure-caked boots against the doorstep, but he soon gave it up for they were all standing in the kitchen in their boots.

"This is Cal Dietz."

Dietz was a bigger man than Roy, over six feet tall and broad. Dietz could sling Roy over his shoulder if he wanted to.

The carrot-headed girl standing next to him stepped forward and held out her hand. Roy read Tully's disapproval in his scowl—too forward for a girl—but she didn't notice.

"I'm Ramona."

With freckles on her nose and a chipped front tooth, she didn't look a day older than sixteen. She grasped his hand and shook it firmly.

"I'm glad to meet you."

"Ramona's Cal's wife," Tully said.

Wife? Dietz had to be thirty years older.

As if Tully meant to squelch any more calculating, he cut in, "Dietz is ready to start right now so you can get the calves weaned. He says Ramona's a good cook."

"I ain't never cooked much before," said Ramona, "but…Mr. Dietz says nobody makes bread as good as I can."

Roy turned to his father to make sense of all this.

"Where'd you find 'em?"

"I went over to the Wrangler and there was Cal, at the bar."

Roy's skepticism must have skittered over his face because Dietz jumped in with more explanation.

"Your dad said he was looking for a ranch hand, and I told him, Mr. Carlton, there's not a better cattleman in this bar than yours truly, but then he went on and said you were the ranch manager and he really needed a ranch couple so the wife could get meals for you, and him, too, when he's out there, and I said, well, Mr. Carlton don't you worry because my wife's right outside in the truck."

Tully met Roy's glare with his own. "If you get going now," he said, "you got just enough time to wean calves before dark."

The image of the child-bride, with her happy, open face, invaded Roy's dreams before daybreak the next morning, and as he crossed the meadow to the bunkhouse, he couldn't shake it from his head. But when he shouldered the door open, the kitchen was dark and coffee hadn't even been started. He shuffled up and down, embarrassed at having to wake a married couple.

"Dietz!" he called finally. He heard the bed creak.

"Coming," Dietz rumbled.

Dietz had pulled on a pair of greasy pants over his union suit. Stubbled skin hung off his jowls.

"Oh. Yeah. Breakfast." He called back to the bedroom. "Mona! Get up!"

Roy sat down at the kitchen table, not knowing what else to do. Dietz lumbered around like a bear, slamming cabinet doors as he looked for the coffee. Silence from the bedroom. Dietz snorted and crossed back to the bedroom doorway.

Roy jumped when he heard, "Get up, you little whore, before I come in there and throw you out! This here's your job!"

The girl scampered out in a flimsy robe that parted at her pale thighs. Roy tried to catch her eyes to see if she felt fear or anger or shame, but she kept her face down. He glanced back at Dietz who dropped into the chair beside him. I should say something to him, thought Roy, but this man was older than him, as old as his father. How could he tell this man how to speak to his wife, even if she looked frail as a fawn?

While he fretted over how he could get it across that he,

Dietz' boss, would appreciate it if he didn't cuss his wife when he was around, coffee appeared before him along with rubbery eggs and burned toast. A new crop of thoughts overgrew the previous ones—had she ever cooked before?

Roy looked up at her, ready to pounce on that question. This time she looked back and glanced quickly over at Dietz. Roy understood. "Don't say anything," she meant, "not in front of him." Roy nodded and scooped some eggs onto his toast.

Dietz's work was passable, but he liked to talk, mostly about himself. He talked about the thousand-head cattle herds he'd managed, the hundreds of sheep he'd sheared in a day's time and all the broncs he'd busted. Roy listened out of politeness, waiting for Dietz to talk about the subject he was interested in: Ramona.

"And when I was working in Sheridan, I was working for Stan Hardigan—ever heard of him?—he runs about two thousand head of purebred Angus, and he raises the meanest bulls I've ever seen, why even the bull calves'll run you down in the weaning pen, get you up against the rail fence and try to nail your balls if..."

"You ever been married before?"

Dietz looked confused. "Married? I 'spose so."

"Ramona isn't your first wife, is she?"

"Oh, no."

"Kids?"

"Oh yeah, a son and a daughter. Their mother ran out on me when we was living in Sinclair. We were on a helluva place out there, a mobile home with no running water. I got stuck out with the herd in a blizzard, and I survived by diggin' a snow cave. You ever done that? I had to let the horse go, and by the time I got back, woman and the kids was gone. I ain't seen 'em since."

"What about Ramona?"

"What about her?"

Roy shrugged. "Just wondered, that's all. Just wonder how…"

"You're married, ain't ya?"

"Yeah."

"You don't like strange men asking questions about your wife, do you?"

Come Sunday morning Roy straightened his bolo tie and pulled on his Western jacket. He looked out at the window, relieved to see the feed truck heading out toward the bunched cattle. You never knew whether the hand would be there or whether he'd be hung over from Saturday night. Dietz was on duty — at least this time.

He turned to watch Fran apply her lipstick in one steady red stroke, the last step in a process of careful pats and dabs that resembled the creation of a masterpiece. She checked first one side of her face, then the other.

As they sauntered through the Country Club dining room, people rose to greet the senior Carltons and Roy's in-laws, the Albrights. Tully Carlton was a short man, but he swelled under people's gazes as he paused here and there to squeeze a shoulder or shake a hand. He expected people to stand when he entered a room. He expected men's hands to be extended. He expected women to rise and cluck over his wife and daughter-in-law.

Only after they were all seated and sipping their coffee and orange juice did Tully bellow from the far end of the table, "How's the help working out?"

Roy glanced up. On his right side was his mother, in her pearls, and Fran. On his left side were Mr. and Mrs. Albright. These women had never met people like Dietz and Ramona.

They wouldn't know what to say to a girl like that. How could he tell them that he suspected Dietz of abuse. They wouldn't know what that was and, he had to admit, he wanted them to stay that way.

"I don't like the way he talks," Roy said finally.

"We're not paying him to talk."

Again, Roy surveyed his audience. "I don't like the way he talks to her."

Maude Albright leaned over her place setting. "You mean his wife?"

"Yes, ma'am."

"What's the matter with it?"

"First of all," Roy paused, "she's a lot younger than him."

"That's not so unusual." Maude offered her explanation to the group, "An older man can be attractive to a younger woman."

"He curses her. He calls her names."

"Maybe she hasn't let him know that she won't tolerate his behavior."

Roy shook his head. "She's...not going to talk like that. She's afraid of him."

"What does this have to do with my cattle?" Tully roared.

"Nothing, Dad. The cattle are fine."

"And he's doing the work?" Tully downed the last of his Bloody Mary.

"Yes."

"And the calves got weaned?"

"Yes."

"Has he been drinking?"

"Not that I've seen."

"And is she cooking?"

Roy considered. "She is real good at homemade bread. That's the best thing she's made so far."

"Sounds like they're working out just fine."

His father-in-law looked on him with pity and said, "You can't judge marriages, Roy. What might sound abrasive to you might be perfectly acceptable to them. Your father's right. As long as they're doing the work, it's not up to you what goes on between them."

"And with vaccinating and dipping coming up, we can't be firing hands because they snap at their wives!" muttered Tully as he sank his fork in his Denver omelet.

"Darling," said Maude, as she laid her jeweled hand down on Roy's, "when will you stop fretting over this ranch and give us a grandbaby?"

Sweat beaded on Roy's forehead. Fran's hands dropped to her lap, and she stared over her mother's chair at the noisy clusters of families beyond. Roy looked down at Maude's diamond, fat as a blood-sated horsefly. With a glance at Tully, he patted her hand. The diamond poked his palm.

"It'll be any day now, any day."

The differences between the family women and Ramona still preoccupied Roy the next morning so that he hardly noticed when Ramona set down his coffee and flapjacks and scuttled back to the bedroom. The speed of her motion made him look up at Dietz.

"Did 'ya have a good day off?" asked Dietz.

Roy nodded. "What about you? How did things go here yesterday?"

"Fine. No problems." He nodded toward the couch. "Napped here all afternoon."

Roy followed his gaze and spied an overturned Jim Beam bottle lying there. Where was she?

"I'd like some more coffee," Roy said.

Dietz pushed his chair away from the table. "I was just going to get myself some. I'll get yours."

He always hollers at her to get the coffee.

18

After breakfast, Roy lingered in the kitchen, thinking that if he waited long enough, she'd appear. Dietz had already opened the outer door. Icy air blasted through the room. Dietz was lacing his boots, pulling on his coat.

Roy blurted, "Where's Ramona this morning?"

"Those damn women things. You know how that goes. Don't you wish you could say to your honey, 'I got the cramps, baby, I can't work.' What do you think she'd say to you, huh?"

Roy nodded. But she'd fixed breakfast.

When they came in at noon, Ramona stood at the stove with her back toward him.

"What's cooking?" Roy called, wanting her to turn around. She didn't.

"Pot roast, potatoes, steamed carrots—and my bread. I know you like that. And I tried a pie this morning."

"Sounds real good."

He expected her smile, but instead, she skulked over to the sink and then slipped out again toward their bedroom.

Dietz did all the serving and they ate in silence. The pie was cherry with whipped cream on top.

"This is really good," Roy said loud enough for Ramona to hear. But the only response he got was Dietz smacking his lips.

That afternoon he sent Dietz to repair the bulls' feed bunk. Ordinarily he would have helped, but he had to see Ramona. He felt guilty circling back to the bunkhouse, squirreling into another man's dwelling when that man was not home, even if it was his own hired hand and the house belonged to the ranch.

He knocked on the door.

"Who is it?"

"It's me, Roy. I'd like another slice of that pie."

"You really liked it?"

"Yeah. I did."

After a pause, she opened the door, but she kept her head down.

"I put a slice on the table for you."

He bent his knees a little, trying to look into her face.

"Aren't you going to sit with me?"

"No. I can't."

"Why not?"

She raised her head, and that's when he saw the black eye. His stomach turned and he swallowed hard.

"How did that happen, Ramona?"

"I went out yesterday to feed with Mr. Dietz. And he told me to get on top of the stack and set them iron hay hooks and he'd winch up the load. And I got on top of the stack and the wind was blowing and the hooks were swinging and they hit me in the head. I look ugly, don't I?"

"No, not ugly, just hurt. Did you put ice on it?"

She nodded and tears pooled in her eyes.

"Are you sure it happened that way?"

"Uh-huh. Don't you believe me?"

He knew she was testing him. If he let his suspicions loose, she'd clam up.

"You need to be more careful. A young girl like you, you shouldn't even be out there."

"I wanted to go."

"Why?"

"I don't want to be stuck in this kitchen all the time."

"We can't be having you out there if you're not careful."

"I'll be careful next time, I promise."

20

"Will you have some pie with me?"

He was pleased when he saw that broad grin break over her face.

"OK. You're sure it's good?"

"It's good."

They sat down together.

"Here," he said. "Let me get you a piece."

They glanced sheepishly at one another as he dished her a huge slice, both conscious that he was serving her instead of the other way round.

She took the plate from him and looked away.

"Thank you."

His chair scraped the floor as he sat down. Forks clinked against the plates while he juggled his questions, thinking how best to pitch them.

She'd eaten all but her crust when he gave up and blurted, "So, how did you meet old Dietz anyway?"

"He came to take care of me when my mama died."

Roy paused. "I'm sorry to hear about that. How long ago has that been?"

"Ten years ago or more. She was crossing the street to the liquor store. I knew she'd been drinking. 'Honey, you stay in the car and wait,' she said, and I knew she shouldn't get out, but I couldn't stop her. She got hit by a truck. And then Mr. Dietz came and got me. And he's taken care of me ever since."

"But you didn't have to marry him."

She stared at him blankly, the one eye crystal blue and the other ringed in bloodish purple. It was as if his statement had wiped her thoughts away.

Then she blurted, "Yes, I had to. Because—you know what? He took me to Vegas. You ever been to Vegas? There's lights everywhere, like a fairyland. We played the slot machines all night 'till I won a jackpot." She giggled. "Those coins poured out like a waterfall, and they filled up my hands, and then his hands, and then they were rolling all over the floor.

"And then he said, 'Ramona, we got enough here for a honeymoon. I know I'm older than you, old enough to be your daddy, and I know how much a young girl wants a good-looking young man, but honey, ain't none of 'em ever going to be true to you like me, take care of you when you're sick, and stay by you forever no matter what.'

"And then, you know what? He got down on his knees." She beamed. "He got down on his knees and then he asked me to be his wife. And then we rode to the wedding chapel in a limousine."

Before Roy could respond, she fired her own question. "Tell me what your wife's like. Fran, that's her name, right?"

"Yes, that's right. She's pretty and smart, and she's a real good cook."

"Good as me?"

"Well, let's say she's cooked a little longer than you."

"I want to meet her someday."

"You will."

"And your daddy—he owns a bank, doesn't he? How come you don't work there?"

"I wouldn't make it chained to a desk. Dad bought this place when I was a kid, and the first day I was here, I rode a horse all day and didn't ever want to go home. Dad's not around much, so this place is all my own."

He felt self-conscious again, this time because of the gaps between them, for Ramona never had a place, never would have one.

He stood up. "I better get out there and get some work done before dark. You take care of that eye, OK?"

She didn't look up at him.

"OK."

Through the night, Roy shuffled scenarios in his mind, looking for a way to confront Dietz without revealing that he'd snuck into the house behind Dietz's back.

The next morning when Ramona tried to hide in the bedroom again, Roy called for her, but she wouldn't come and Dietz spouted the same excuses. Three days later, she finally sat down with them at breakfast. The bruising around her eye had turned snot green.

With a quick glance at Dietz, Roy asked, "What happened to you?"

"Uh..."

Dietz jumped in before she could answer. "She helped me last Sunday when you was in town and hit herself in the head with the hay hooks." Dietz shook his head and chuckled. "That's some shiner she's got now."

"Those hay hooks are too heavy for a woman to handle. Maybe you'd better not take her out there again."

"It's not like you're paying her."

"I just don't want her to get hurt, that's all."

Dietz eyed him. "Is that an order?"

Roy felt prodded to rise to the challenge. "Yeah."

"Sorry, honey, you're not going to be able to go out with me again. You heard the man."

Ramona looked hurt, as if Roy himself had struck her. Dietz smirked.

That night at supper, Fran said, "I got this recipe out of the newspaper. How do you like it?"

He directed his attention to the hamburger-macaroni casserole. To tell the truth, he had hardly tasted it because he'd been working on how to ask her to befriend Ramona.

"It's great, honey."

"More?"

"You bet," and he held out his plate. He watched her rise and walk to the stove. When her back was turned, he started, "Honey?"

"Hmmm."

"Are you going to town next week?"

"It's a silly question. Of course I am. Why are you asking?"

"You got plans?"

She looked back at him. "I've got a hair appointment and bridge club in the afternoon. You're never interested in what I do in town. Why now?"

"I was wondering if you could take Ramona with you."

"Ramona? What for?"

"She wants to meet you. She's all alone in that house, and she doesn't have any friends, and I just thought..." His wife was glaring at him. "You could be a friend to her, that's all."

"She's the cook, Roy."

He aimed for another angle.

"You know what it's like out here. Think what it's like for a young girl married to an old man."

"I know what it's like. I know what it is to sit here day after day listening to the wind and waiting for you to get home to talk about your cows and your father. I know all about that. I know all about being alone. You're never this concerned about me. Why are you worrying about her?"

"She can't get away."

"She married him, didn't she? She must have known what she was getting into."

"I don't know."

"Well, Roy, I don't know why you would ask me such a thing. How would it look—me chauffeuring the ranch cook around town?"

"You've never even met her. You've never even gone over there and introduced yourself."

"Why should I? She's the help!"

Fran was right, of course. He thought back to the Albrights' Labor Day cocktail party last fall, how lovely Fran had looked in her evening dress as the sun set and the yard lights snapped on. He'd dropped his conversation just to watch her. How proud he'd felt that she belonged to him. How could he expect her to pull on overshoes, smash a hood over her hair and tromp through the snow to sit at the grimy table and listen to Ramona talk about Las Vegas and slot machines. How could he have imagined that?

She set the steaming plate in front of him.

"I'm sorry, Fran."

She sat down quietly and didn't answer.

He reached across the table and squeezed her hand.

"I don't know what I'd do without you."

The tension in her jaw relaxed.

"Can you sleep in tomorrow?"

"Honey, you know I can't. We're feeding."

While he pitched hay to the horses the next morning, Ramona joined him wearing a moth-chewed plaid coat. Her curls blew about her face in the stiff breeze. She stepped gingerly around the manure.

"Can I pat the horses?" she asked.

"Sure."

She walked over to the closest one, took off her mittens and sank her fingers in his thick winter hair. The sensation brought an instant grin to her face.

"You like horses?"

"I love 'em." She ran her hands over the horse's withers and down his spine.

"You ever had a horse?"

She shook her head, "No, but Mr. Dietz says soon as we settle down, he'll get me one."

"Do you know how to ride?"

"Yes. Mr. Dietz taught me."

"Well, maybe come calving, you could ride with us."

"I'd love that. Can I feed 'em?"

"Sure." He handed her the pitchfork. She was awkward forking hay, but it gave her such pleasure that he let it go.

"You want to give 'em some cake?"

She nodded.

He brought out half a bucket of cottonseed cake from the barn and gave it to her. Most women would have been scared by so many large animals crowding in on them, but she laughed as they snatched the cake from her hand.

"Roy, can I feed them every day?"

"You mean the hay?"

"Yes."

"That's one less chore for me. Sure."

Dietz saw them in the lot and leaned over the gate.

"What are you two doing here?"

"Roy's going to let me feed the horses from now on."

"He is?" Dietz looked at Roy. "That's mighty nice."

"And he says I can go riding come calving season."

Watching Dietz's face cloud over, Roy realized the rashness of his offer.

"I thought you said you didn't want her out here."

Roy squirmed, pinned between Ramona's expectations and Dietz' disapproval.

"Pitching hay here by the house is a lot safer than setting hooks on a haystack in the wind."

Dietz glared at him.

"And it's a pretty good while between now and calving."

To avoid Dietz, he glanced at Ramona. She went from one horse to the other, rubbing their heads. They nosed her for more cake.

"You're the boss," said Dietz.

The Widow Smalls and Other Stories

On Thanksgiving, Dietz was to feed and then take the rest of the day off. Roy and Fran were going to town, where they'd have brunch with her parents and supper with his. Roy slowed as they drove past the ranch house.

"What?" said Fran.

"Just checking to make sure Dietz is doing his job."

There were tracks where the feed truck had pulled out, so everything was all right. He thought of Ramona. Tully had brought out a Thanksgiving turkey with all the trimmings, so she should have a good day. Maybe.

At night when they came home, Dietz's truck was gone. Maybe they'd gone out, he thought.

The next morning Dietz was alone in the kitchen frying the eggs.

"Morning," he said to Roy.

"Morning."

Where was Ramona? Roy listened for a rustle, a step, a sigh, anything that would tell him where she was, but the house was silent.

Dietz set the platter of eggs on the table.

"Have a good Thanksgiving?" he asked.

"Yes. Yourself?"

"Very nice. We appreciated that turkey."

Roy reached for the toast, his anxiety about Ramona shooting from the floor of his stomach, up his windpipe.

"Ramona sleeping late this morning?"

Dietz sighed before he spoke. "I thought I'd let her sleep in. We had to go to the hospital after dinner yesterday. She broke her arm."

"Broke her arm? How?"

"She went skating on the river and fell."

"I didn't know she could skate."

Dietz dipped two pieces of toast in the yolk on his plate.

"She's a good skater. Just hit a bump, that's all. Guess she won't be feeding horses for a while."

"Are you sure that's what happened?"

Dietz's eyebrows arched. "What d'ya mean?"

"I mean I think you broke her arm."

Dietz snorted. "You got some kinda imagination, kid."

"I think you gave her the black eye, too."

"Really? And what are you going to do about it? Call your daddy?"

"If she gets hurt again, I'll call the sheriff."

Roy jumped as Dietz threw his chair back from the table. Dietz stomped off to the bedroom and Roy could hear the voices, Dietz telling her to get up and her voice in reply, sleepy, pouty. He heard the mattress springs creak and the voices again, more subdued. She came into the dining room in the frayed silk robe, her curls flattened against her head and her arm in a cast. She looked at Roy and sat down heavily.

"Roy wants to know how you broke your arm."

"I fell on the ice."

"What were you doing?"

"Skating. I was ice-skating."

Dietz took the coffee pot off the stove. "I guess you got time for another cup, Roy, now that you don't have so many phone calls to make."

Tully said they'd dip the cows the first week of December, but Roy didn't want to put it off till then. The weather was balmy that last week of November, and he knew any day the winter blizzards would come.

He tried coaxing: "Let's not wait another week. With the weather this warm, it won't be so hard on the cows."

"We've always done it in December."

"What if we get a storm and the corrals drift in?"

"We'll shovel 'em out."

Just as Roy feared, the sky was slate gray on the day before dipping. The wind blew sharp and low clouds scuttled overhead. Tully came out to supervise the preparation of the vat and corrals. He watched while Roy and Dietz mixed barrel after barrel of pesticide and water and poured it in the vat.

"Pewey!" said Dietz. "That stuff smells bad enough to kill more than lice. Seems like just the stench of it could kill a cow, too."

"Lice is all we need it to kill. The cows'll be all right," muttered Tully.

"Aren't they going to freeze to death in that stuff?"

"No. That's why they got fur."

"But we have lost a few," volunteered Roy.

"How?"

"This cage lowers down into the vat. And we use the truck to raise and lower the cage. So if the driver doesn't keep the tension tight on the cable, the cow'll drown in the vat."

"That's happened?"

"It's happened when we've had the hands driving," snapped Tully. "Now just Roy does the driving."

Dietz grinned. "Good thing."

Roy woke at three a.m. the next morning. He sat up for a moment and listened. The wind was low, just the faintest keening around the corners of the house. He walked to the front door and turned on the yard light. Sheets of snow were swirling and falling, swirling and falling again. Five inches—already!— on the ground. He lay back down in bed. Fran snuggled deeper into the covers, pulling the quilt over her head. Roy stared at the ceiling and braced for the coming day.

The wind was howling when he got up at five. Tully, who'd spent the night, was already up. He stood at the kitchen window, staring into the darkness. Roy spotted the empty shot glass on the table. The odor of Scotch lingered in the room.

"Got a little storm going out there," Tully said.

"Yeah. You ready?"

They trudged through the snow to the bunkhouse. Ramona, at the stove, grinned when Tully came in.

"Good morning, Mr. Carlton. How ya doing?" She laid out slices of bacon in the skillet.

"What did you do to your arm?"

Dietz looked at Roy. "She broke it ice-skating."

"She can still cook though, can't she?"

"Yes, Mr. Carlton," she answered, "Here's your coffee."

They sat down at the table and waited, five minutes, then ten. "Where's breakfast?" Tully said loudly.

Ramona quickly set down platters of bacon, scrambled eggs, hash browns and oatmeal and toast.

Tully pushed the hash browns away in disgust.

"These aren't done enough."

"She can do you some more," Dietz offered.

"We don't have time," Tully growled, and he reached for the oatmeal. "Roy—you and Dietz are going to have to shovel out the corrals. I'll be along with the cows. Then we'll all load the chute. Roy'll do the lowering, like I said. I'll do the vaccinations and load the cage. Dietz, you'll have to keep 'em coming up through the chute."

Dietz's mouth was full. "Got it," he mumbled.

As they filed out the door, Tully turned back to Ramona.

"What time did you get up this morning, young lady?"

"Five, sir."

"And you couldn't fry hash browns by six. What are you, retarded?"

Ramona's face paled.

Roy spoke up, "She's only got one arm, Dad. She's doing the best she can."

Tully didn't take his eyes off the girl. "I expect she'll do better next time."

She turned away. Roy struggled to find something to say, anything to blunt the impact, but Tully and Dietz were already out the door and there was nothing he could do.

"I'm sorry," he said, "My dad's just...we got a long day ahead and it's already a blizzard out there."

"You said this was your own place, Roy, so why do you let your daddy talk that way?"

"Why do you let Dietz whop on you?"

She faced him and he caught his breath as she seemed to teeter on the edge of spilling the truth. Just give her one more second and she'd utter the words that he could use to save her from Dietz. *C'mon Ramona.* But instead, she shook her curls, flinging the thought away.

"I bet Fran's real pretty. I look out every morning and see your brick house and think about how nice it must be. It'd be better if you stayed over there."

"Tell me! Now!"

Tully bellowed, "Roy—you gonna cling to that girl's apron strings all day?"

He was so close—he knew he could pry it out of her but there was no time. "I got to be going," he muttered and left.

The work went slow, but at least in the truck Roy kept warmer than either Dietz or Tully. One by one the cows were prodded into the vat and lowered. They came up streaming wet, icicles forming on their sides. They dripped off on the cement pad and then Dietz turned them back out into the pasture where they disappeared in the whiteout.

Visibility—that was a problem. The snow flew so thick that Roy could barely see between the truck and the vat. He didn't dare take his eyes off of Tully's hand signals.

Noon came and went. Tully said they'd work on through so as to get done by dark. At two p.m., it seemed as if the light was already waning.

Without a word, Tully slammed the cage door shut and ran down the chute. Something had happened. Roy stepped outside. Snow pelted his face and the blast of wind nearly took his breath away. He followed his father's tracks into the corral. Dietz was lying on the ground and Tully was beside him.

"What happened?"

"Cow knocked him and stepped on his foot."

"I think it's broken!" Dietz screamed.

"Let's get him up," said Tully. They leaned him up against the rails. Dietz blew, heaving like a bull, and threw his head back.

"Can you put weight on it?" asked Tully.

"No, I can't."

Tully and Roy looked at one another. "We oughtta quit," said Roy.

"We can't quit. If we let 'em all go, we won't know which cows we've done and which we haven't."

"We could hold the rest here in the corrals overnight."

"How would they get water?"

Tully was right. There was no way they could haul water to the corrals.

"Which foot is it?" said Tully.

"My right one," groaned Dietz.

"You think you could drive?"

"I think so. Why?"

"So you could operate the cage and we could finish up?"

"I think so."

They helped Dietz to the truck, and once they got him loaded, Tully said, "Do you understand what to do?"

"Yeah, go forward lowers the cage. Reverse raises it."

It was four o'clock now and the yard lights were coming on. Snow swirled over the mass of huddled cows.

Into the cage. Then down. Then up. Roy was numb to everything but the headlights. Then the truck stalled.

Tully yelled, "Get it started back up! Quick!"

Roy ran to the front of the truck. It had jerked forward and the cable was slack.

Roy shouted along with Tully, "Quick! Quick! Get moving."

The truck started and Dietz gunned it back. They watched as the cage rose. Roy was relieved to see the cow standing, but then her knees buckled and she went down. Roy threw open the gate as if that would save her. She was already gone. Her head lolled on to the cement pad.

"Goddammit! Goddammit! Goddammit!" Tully screamed.

Dietz tried to talk. "It's just...I'm getting tired and no food and the pain..."

"Get on home! Get out of here!"

"He can't get home, Dad. We need the truck to haul this cow out of here. And there's twenty cows left to do."

"He can damn well walk!"

Roy helped Dietz out of the truck and walked him away from his father's hearing.

"Dad left the feed truck outside of the corrals when he brought the cows in. Do you think you can drive that home?"

Dietz panted, as if he'd been running.

"Your father's a powerful man, Roy. Him and me— we're both powerful men. Oh, I'd be his equal if I had all that money."

Roy grimaced and turned away.

"Oh, I'd have me a ranch and cattle and I'd hire two-bit piss ants to run it, too."

"You better get home, Dietz."

"God, if I didn't have this bad foot, I woulda pulled back and broke his jaw!"

It was then that Roy remembered Ramona waiting alone at the house, hour after hour with the noon meal grown cold. He thought of her doll chin lifting as Dietz lumbered in.

"I can't get you to the hospital tonight," Roy said. "In the morning, we'll try, if we can make it out of here."

"I ain't going to the hospital," Dietz said. "I've been hurt a lot worse 'n this. Ol' Dietz'll be just fine." Roy loaded him into the feed truck. The engine roared, the lights came on and Dietz headed up the road.

He'll get drunk and sleep it off, thought Roy.

He didn't think of Ramona again until he woke at five the next morning. He listened. Silence. He and Tully had eaten the warmed leftovers Fran fixed for them the night before and had gone to bed without another word.

He dressed quietly and tiptoed past the guest room. Tully was snoring. No point in waking him up. Roy had turned the cows out and they didn't need Tully anymore. He and Dietz could feed by themselves.

The snow was powdery underfoot and gleaming in the last light from the sickle moon. The whole world was dead, even the stars were frozen solid. The only sound of life was the blood thumping in his ears.

Dietz's truck was gone. The tracks went out of the barnyard, down the road and disappeared in the murk. He'd probably quit, thought Roy. He'd probably left for good.

Still he kept walking to the bunkhouse. The sagging door was open and a breath emanated from the house, tinged with the odor of musty cupboards. He stepped inside. The kitchen was dark and cold.

"Ramona!" he called out, but no one answered. He hesitated, then stepped into the bedroom. The dawn light reflected in the mirror on top of the bureau and he looked down at scattered belongings: beads, hair clips, a brush trailing red hairs—and a photograph. He picked it up. It was Dietz as a younger man, his torso slimmer, his hair dark and full. He wore a tee-shirt with the sleeve rolled over a pack of cigarettes. Sitting on his lap was a child—Ramona—in a princess dress with her hair pulled back and curled around her face. One of his hands held her gently at the abdomen and the other stroked her neck.

He took the photograph with him back out to the kitchen and sat down. Tully walked in.

Roy tossed the photograph in front of him. "You seen this?"

Tully sat down and took off his hat. He looked stony, the way he'd look before telling someone he was foreclosing on their property, so that their reaction would hit the wall of his gaze and run down.

"You mean you didn't know she was the daughter."

Roy exploded, "You knew? And you didn't say anything?"

"You've been letting that man rattle in your ear for weeks and you were too dumb to figure it out?"

"I knew he was hurting her! I was trying to get her to say it! That way, I could've done something to stop him! She was about to tell me yesterday and then you…"

"Me? Stomping in manure is where you belong, son, because you can't manage in the real world. All that woman'll ever be is some man's cook or whore."

"Because of you! You and Dietz! That's what you two made of her!"

Tully snorted, "Listen to you. You wanted her, too!"

Roy leaped up and grabbed the phone.

"What are you doing?"

"Sheriff?"

"What the hell are you calling the Sheriff for?"

"This is Roy Carlton."

Tully grabbed his arm. Roy jerked it away.

"Get away from me!"

"Roy," said the Sheriff, "what's going on?"

He heard the familiar click of another phone lifting to another ear.

"Listen…Ms. Strader, you got to get off this line."

Silence.

He screamed. "Get off the line!"

35

Click. She was gone.

"Roy?"

"Something's happened here. We had a girl working for us. A man, Cal Dietz, said he was her husband. But he wasn't. He was her father. He was sleeping with his own daughter."

He and Tully glared at one another while the Sheriff questioned him in a voice sinking back into sleep. Did they come from around here? Where were they now? Did he know where they'd gone? He paused and Roy imagined him looking at his clock.

"What did you want me to do, Roy?"

Roy hung up the phone.

He turned and left his father standing there. He would find them. Dietz probably hadn't gone farther than the bar where Tully had found him. Maybe when Ramona realized that he'd come after her, she'd see this wasn't the way it had to be. Who knows? Maybe they'd both escape their fathers.

He jumped into the four-wheel drive pickup and roared out of the yard. Dietz's tracks were half-drifted over. He rammed snowdrift after snowdrift and the truck fish-tailed through. The highway was just ahead. If Dietz had made it this far, he could, too. He hit the accelerator hard to go through the last drift, but it was too long and too high and the truck shuddered to a halt.

He rocked it back and forth. Nothing. He was just spinning. He grabbed the shovel from the truck bed. After twenty minutes, he managed to rock it forward a foot or two. Then it was stuck again. *Dammit!* How had Dietz made it through this?

He threw his coat in the truck bed and shoveled again. He shoveled and rocked, shoveled and rocked, until with one last shimmy, the tires broke through and the truck rested, rumbling on the asphalt.

Curls of vapor rolled off the blacktop, sandwiched as it was between banks of snow, like a river winding away from him. He thought of the rivers at flood stage in the spring, how they swept the banks in one smacking roar, carrying all the scrap miles downstream beyond the borders of his geography.

Through the windshield, the sky arched ice-blue, tauntingly empty.

He circled the truck back around, back through the tracks he'd made to where a woman waited by a window, where cattle waited, with their ears pricked for the rumble of the feed truck, where an old man waited who would scowl with satisfaction when he arrived.

He drove up to his house, left his boots and coveralls in the mudroom and went inside.

"Roy?" Fran called, "Is that you? Tully's out feeding. He said Dietz quit. He said you went to look for him. Did you find him?"

"No."

"I'm making a Christmas wreath. Do you want to see it?"

He trailed her into the living room. Their Christmas tree was in the corner, smothered in tinsel and blinking lights. A few gaudy boxes were already littered underneath the boughs. The wreath lay on the dining room table, woven through with red and white ribbons, sprigs of mistletoe and silver balls.

She looked into his face.

"What do you think?"

His gaze drifted up over her plucked eyebrows, to her forehead, white as a new snowdrift, with only the faintest of lines. He pulled her to him, inhaled her perfume.

"It's beautiful."

Jamie Lisa Forbes

Lincoln's Nephew

Jamie Lisa Forbes

The Widow Smalls and Other Stories

Lawrence Yarborough *parked himself at the table with his coffee. No escaping now. It didn't matter if you had the noon pot roast burning in your oven. You weren't going anywhere until you'd heard him out.*

Ranch hands. Time was when you couldn't manage with 'em and you couldn't manage without 'em. Now we got the kids. They've growed to where at least they know to hop out of the gate when you're driving a herd of cattle straight at 'em. But there's room for improvement.

Like Ray for instance. You heard how he tried to cross the Pioneer ditch on the three-wheeler, didn't ya? That ditch drops straight down ten feet and comes up straight ten feet on the other side. Well, Ray musta watched too much of that *Dukes a Hazzard* show, I guess, 'cause he goes buzzing down one bank and as he buzzes up the opposite bank, the thing flips back on top of him and down he slides right into the creek bed. If the game warden hadn't a come along and extracted him, he'd be there yet.

The warden was out hazing the hunters who were out

hazing the antelope. And what does he come up with? A three-wheeler in the ditch with its wheels spinning round and Ray under it pawing the air like a beetle flipped on its back. That's just what I mean about Ray—he don't anticipate.

But kids with no sense is still better than ranch hands. Oh, you might land a man with some savvy all right, but where was he when you needed him? Parked on a stool at the Cowboy Bar. Haying was the worst, 'cause instead of one or two to contend with, you had fifteen or twenty. A 'course that was in the days when folks still hayed with teams.

I've seen 'em all come and go, but I never met any like Lincoln's nephew. That's right! Abe Lincoln's nephew worked right here, right on this place. Don't get that smirk like I'm pullin' your leg! Well, maybe he was a grandnephew or something, since it'd been seventy years or so since Lincoln died.

That feller looked just like Lincoln. He had the same craggy face and long nose, and he even parted his hair on the same side.

When we first laid eyes on him—my little brother, James, and me—he was crossing the hay meadow. We stopped what we was doing 'cause it looked as if a telephone pole had grown legs. Collar bone on him was high as the crown of Dad's head.

When he dropped his canvas bag at Dad's feet, we couldn't stand ourselves no more. James charged right up to him and craned his neck all the way back, though he couldn't see more than the whiskers on his chin.

I hung back with Dad.

His flannel shirt was sweat-stained and ripped at the elbows and then, his shirttails flapped out over his pants. Dad huffed a little and we checked our own shirts. No excuse for sloppiness in a man, no matter which president he took after.

I knew what the real Lincoln looked like, so I thought I was seeing a ghost. Lincoln, the real one, hung in our schoolhouse. The glass was cracked all the way across his picture, but no doubt he was frowning. Those eyes burrowed into our heads and read all those schemes we cooked up to make the day go by. Maybe a squirrel stuffed down the stove pipe or cow pies in a girl's seat. Lincoln never took his eyes off of us. Year after year, he kept a frowning and frowning.

And now, here he'd showed up with his shirttails hanging out. Dad's frown didn't seem to register on him. He pulled a kerchief from his pocket and mopped his brow. Then he held out his hand.

"Afternoon, Mr. Yarborough. My name's Lincoln."

We gasped. But Dad didn't have no more reaction than if he'd been any regular feller bringing out the mail. He shook Lincoln's hand and stepped back.

"What can I do for you?"

"I heard you need a little extra help to finish haying."

Dad glanced back down at them shirttails. "You ever hayed before, Mr. Lincoln?"

Lincoln nodded. "I know you're thinking I don't amount to much, but I've been up and down this country for quite some time now. I can do any ranch work, except cowboying. I never could stay in the saddle and I've given up on it."

"Up and down this country, you say. Why's that?"

Lincoln shrugged. "A feller likes to test himself in the world, I guess."

Dad's eyes traveled out across the standing hay, balancing how much we had left to cut against the odds that this Lincoln could so much as heft a pitchfork. The time dripped by while that sun beat down on us hotter and hotter. I wanted to make a beeline for the creek, and I know James did too, but the suspense kept us glued to the ground, sweating right alongside those men.

"Tuck in that shirt," Dad said finally. "Then getch'ya a pitchfork and start topping out that stack out there."

Wouldn't you know, there was Lincoln scrambling to mash those shirttails down them pants.

It troubled me over the next week or so, trying to splice this Lincoln feller with that picture on the schoolhouse wall. Who was who? Then again, I wasn't sure I wanted to know. No tellin' what I'd learn 'bout either one of 'em if I started poking around.

One evening after supper, I decided it was now or never, so I walked right up to him and said, "How come you ain't in that White House?"

He was sitting in a rocker on the porch of the bunkhouse plunkin' a banjo. He didn't stop right away. He kept twangin' his tune while I fidgeted, then he took his kerchief out real slow and took forever to wipe that banjo down.

"Oh, I been there," he said.

My jaw dropped so wide a cloud of mosquitoes near choked me. "You have?"

He nodded. "Uh-huh. What do you want to know about it?"

"Well," —start with basics, that's what I thought— "What's it like inside?"

"All white. Walls, floors, ceilings, everything. About as white-washed as paradise."

My questions all piled up on me. Wasn't we 'sposed to want to be in paradise, to aim for it? The way he was sounding, it was the last place a feller'd want to be.

But instead, I asked, "What were you doing there?"

"They took me to see my uncle."

"You mean Abraham Lincoln?"

"'Course I mean Abraham Lincoln. There ain't been no Lincolns in the White House since then."

"Well, what did he say?"

"Fact is, they took me to see him because I was a scoundrel and they thought he could talk some sense into me. You might not know, but he was kind of famous for talking."

"What happened?"

"They led me through a set of white double doors and

then down a long white hall. I was glad my boots were muddy, 'cause naturally them floors were white, and I wanted to leave a little something of myself behind.

We got to the end and they led me through another set of white double doors. And there was Abraham Lincoln. He sat in a big crickety rocking chair, just like this one. Behind him on that white wall were pictures of all the presidents: Washington, Jefferson, Jackson—all of 'em. They were all looking down at me. And Lincoln sat there rocking in his old chair and frowning."

That sounded like Lincoln, as far as I knew him.

"Then what?"

"He opened his mouth and said, 'Son, the Rebel flag'll be draped in this office 'fore you ever amount to somethin', so if I was you, I wouldn't even bother to try.'"

"That's all he said?"

"That's it."

"Didn't you ever want to be president?"

"Nope."

"Why not?"

"I see it as kinda restrictive. Beholden to all, freedom for none. The world owns you. You can't never return to who you knew you were."

I thought back on the picture at the schoolhouse. Whatever else he thought, that Lincoln seemed satisfied with himself, near as I could tell.

Along in the fall after haying, Lincoln asked for two days off to go to town. I just sunk listening to it. You know yourself, when a hand says he's going to town for two days, it's likely to mean you ain't never gonna see him again. Without Lincoln to spy on and think about, ranch life was going to lose its intrigue.

But two days later, here he come while we were out

45

mending the corral. I couldn't contain myself a'tall, and in spite a Dad's frowning, I pounded down that dirt road hard as I could. I flew smack into Lincoln's knees just boiling over with questions about where he'd been and what he'd been doing.

He looked pretty ragged, a lot worse than the first time we'd seen him. He had a couple stitches under his eye, his whiskers had grown in and his shirttails was out again. He didn't pay me no mind. He brushed me off, as if I wasn't more than a horsefly. It busted me up that he wouldn't talk to me, so I near hung on them shirttails all the way to the bunkhouse door.

He put his hand on the knob and said, "I know you mean to welcome me back, and on another day, I'd appreciate it, but it's wasted effort today."

"What'cha mean?" I asked.

"I mean my stay here might be cut short—involuntarily." Then he went in and shut the door.

And not more than two hours later, here come the mud-colored Sheriff's car lumbering down the road. I run and got James and we near fainted from the spectacle. In those days, the Sheriff driving out all the way from town was the same as if the Archangel Gabriel came down, fluttered his wings and blew his horn in the yard.

The Sheriff got out of the car, and we hemmed and hawed while he and Dad exchanged the preliminaries about what a mild season it was and what each one supposed the other thought about what kinda winter we could expect, and you wondered why a feller'd drive thirty-seven miles to talk such nonsense when the Sheriff said, "I hear you got a hand here, a Mr. Lincoln."

"He just got back from town," Dad said.

"I wished he'd stayed put and saved me the trip out. He's passed bad checks at all the watering holes."

"You know your business, Sheriff. I got plenty of my own and these boys," he nodded his chin towards us, "could do without further distraction."

"I'll get to it then," said the Sheriff. He rapped on the bunkhouse door and called out, "Lincoln, you come out here."

And then—to our pure rapture—he unholstered his revolver.

But Lincoln didn't put up no fight a 'tall. He drug outta the bunkhouse, his hair flopping over his eyes, and he stood there all dejected while the Sheriff handcuffed him, and then it took a few minutes to fold all of him into the car and then they were gone, kicking a cloud a dust behind 'em.

Dad turned back to the corral as if nothing out of the ordinary had happened. He looked at us.

"I don't feed you boys to gawk in the road," he said.

He picked up a nail and drove it through a post with one smack of his hammer.

That fall, my granddad had given me a new pen knife. I hadn't ever had a knife before, so I thought this one was the dandiest I'd ever seen. It had an ivory handle and three or maybe four blades. I used to pull 'em out all at one time, just to make sure they were all there. A 'course, I was warned not to take that knife to school, but what's the use of a fancy knife like that if a feller can't show it to his friends? I waited till one day when James threw up his breakfast and Mama couldn't quite concentrate on what I was up to. Then I slipped that knife into my pocket and went off to school.

Well, you know Kenny Randolph, don't you? He owns the place down the creek. I never have cared for him much. Work don't scare him none—he can curl up and snore right next to it. After school that day, Kenny and I were walking home. He had a dumb grin on his face. He's still got that grin, but he gets it outta whiskey bottles now.

He says, "Why don't you show me your knife again?"

'Course, I'd been showing my knife around all day long.

I put my hand in my pocket and it wasn't there. I stopped walking and Kenny stopped. I was searching all my pockets till Kenny said, "Looking for this?" and I seen my prize possession in his fat hand.

"Give it here," I said.

"Finders, keepers."

That skunk hadn't found it, he'd snitched it right outta my pocket! I jumped on him and started pounding. Then I kicked and scratched every part of him I could reach. There weren't more things in this world that one body can do to another that I didn't want to do to Kenny. If I coulda managed it, I'd a knocked him senseless and thrown him in the creek.

But I missed my chance, because right about then two big hands picked me up and set me on the ground. I looked up and there was Lincoln!

"Lincoln, how'd you get outta jail? Did you escape?"

"Never mind that. You better get on home."

He yanked Kenny to his feet. Kenny was crying, a 'course. Then Lincoln spun me around and we walked away, leaving fat Kenny crying in the road.

I trudged beside him, rubbing my bruises 'till I remembered something was missing.

"You got my knife?"

He opened up his hand, but before I could grab it, his hand closed round it again.

"I know in light of my recent adversities, I ain't the type to set an example for you," he said, "but to the casual observer, you need to reflect on what it was you were advertisin' when you carried that knife in your back pocket, where everyone could see it and reach it. Seems like that fight was something you aimed for all along."

"If they can't see it, they ain't going to believe I have it."

"What did they need to know for? It didn't improve no

one's day, did it? I've been dang near suffocated all my life by men advertising how big they were. Big houses, big cars, wads of money. Here's what I know: the more of a load a man packs to show how big he is, well, it's just a sign of how little he makes of himself on the inside. And if he thinks he's small, then what is anyone else to make of him?"

He stopped then and looked down at me. "So you study on it, what are we to make of you."

"Can we study on that after I get my knife back?"

We were at the bunkhouse door and he didn't say nothing more. He just closed the door on my nose.

I went on into the house. The cuckoo clock crowed the hour, and there was Dad at the dining room table with a stack of bills and his big old ledger books in front of him. He didn't hardly look up.

"From the sight of you, the field of education was not advanced today."

That mightta been true, but with his head stuck in them books, he'd missed out on the big news.

"Lincoln's escaped from jail," I said. "He's back in the bunkhouse."

Dad pushed his bifocals back on his forehead. "I posted his bail."

I glanced over at the clock 'cause it seemed like it shoulda stopped dead on the wall! I tried to picture it, Dad at the jail plunkin' down money to free Lincoln. It was easier to picture the pigs a flyin'.

But no, the clock kept on tick-tocking and Dad looked up again.

"Devil's liable to cut the tongue from a mouth hangin' open. You got wood to chop out back, that is if you want dinner."

"Why'd you do it, Dad?"

He put down his pencil and sighed. "Well, I kinda like listenin' to that banjo every now and then. He's an oddity alright, but I believe there's a vein of decency in him. Every man's got some decency deep down, even if he's spoilt like you and your brother. I wanted to give him a chance and see if he'd turn out to do good in some way. I'll regret it, most likely."

Sometime in May, when the grass had turned green, but the trees were still bare, Lincoln and I cleaned out the barn. Lincoln found an old English saddle up in the hayloft. He hauled it out in the sunlight. He set it on a saddle stand and polished that thing 'till the reflection off the leather 'bout blinded a feller.

"What're you doing with that?" I asked him. Why would he be fussin' so much over a saddle when he didn't ride?

Lincoln just muttered, "It needed it," and he went right on working.

That following Sunday was a warm day. A breeze come up from the south and blew ripples in the mud puddles in the yard. After Sunday dinner, I stepped out of the house to mess around on my own. As I came round the corner of the barn, I met up with a sight every bit as fantastic as the Sheriff driving in the front yard.

Lincoln was out in the pasture. He was riding a big sorrel colt, one that Dad had been breaking for himself. Dad had grained that colt throughout the winter and brushed him every day 'till he gleamed. James and me and Mama and the hands and the whole world, as far as I knew, had been told not to touch that colt, but there was Lincoln on that old English saddle. He had that big colt loping round and round, as smooth as the creek in midsummer. For a man who told us he couldn't stay in the saddle, he must have caught on fast, because he looked as if he was fixing to lead a charge of the Union cavalry.

But what set me wondering was the contraption Lincoln had set up in the center of the pasture. He'd placed two barrels opposite one another with some poles across the top. I was about to shout out to him when Lincoln reined the horse straight towards the thing. I was expecting a wreck, but that horse just flew over those poles as sure of himself as if he'd been doing it all his life. My heart near shot out my windpipe just watching it!

I ran out to the pasture, shouting, "Hey Lincoln! Show me how to do that!"

But before he could stop, that colt threw down his head and bucked so hard his back feet nearly brushed the clouds with every stride. You'd a thought a feller would lose his seat at the first jump in that English saddle, but Lincoln hung on and hung on until they smacked into the barbed wire fence and toppled over.

Dad was there by that time and we run out to the two of them. Both of 'em were tore up by the barbed wire, blood gushing down the colt's legs and Lincoln's forehead.

All you could hear was the chorus of spring peepers. But they plumb hushed when Dad spoke.

"You didn't tell me quite right, Lincoln. Seems you've done a fair amount of cowboying in your time. "

Lincoln sat up and wiped the blood off the bridge of his nose.

"As you see for yourself — not quite enough."

Dad nodded. "The horse could've been spared."

Lincoln struggled to his feet and looked down on Dad.

"You got a right to be mad, Yarborough, and I'm sorry. You folks have treated me right. It was sore temptation, admiring that colt day after day, every bit as bad as a whiskey bottle. It's always temptation that's goaded me, making me think the whole world'll crack open for me if I just squeeze it a little bit harder.

"I'll go get my things together."

"That'd be all right," said Dad.

Lincoln walked a few steps and then stopped again. He turned, reached into his pocket and held out my knife.

I looked down at it, laying in his palm and said, "I don't think I want it no more."

He knelt down, put it in my hand and closed my fingers around it.

"Look on it next time you think you want something and you'll remember what a fickle, troublesome ol' feller Desire really is."

None of us ever mentioned him again. I puzzled about it, where he'd really come from and why he'd come to us. But as you know yourself, you can't keep frettin' over those that have blown on into the wide world. It's too much a waste of a feller's sap.

Another year and a few months passed. It was haying season again. I was working my own team by then. We'd just finished breakfast and the whole hay crew was headed out to the meadow. The sun was bright in that old dusty yard, just as it is out there right now, 'cept that day happened fifty years ago.

The air was snappy. Autumn's claw was already prying into the year. Still, you could smell that fresh mown hay.

I'd set my mind on the hot day ahead when a big shiny car pulled into the yard. More than a car — a limousine. It came to a dead stop and a driver in a uniform stepped out and opened up the back door and out stepped Lincoln's nephew. He turned, held out his hand, and tugged out a pudgy lady with a mop of red curls sticking out from under a little pink hat.

Lincoln's attitude about advertising musta changed 'cause he was wearing the kind of suit fellers get buried in, and he had a gold watch chain in his vest pocket and shiny black shoes without a smudge on 'em. His shirttails was tucked in, I noticed.

It was so quiet in that yard, you could a heard the dew dry. The redheaded woman kinda bumped her hip against his leg and grabbed his arm. Her face twitched like she'd walked into a herd of wild buffalo and couldn't believe what she was seeing. 'Course I'd never seen anything like her. Up 'til that day, I don't recall that I'd ever seen a woman with lipstick, much less lipstick the color of fresh blood.

The hands that were there hadn't ever seen Lincoln's nephew before. Their eyes were big as billiard balls, 'cause with his hair combed and his face cleaned, Lincoln's nephew looked more like the President than ever.

James tore off toward the house to get Mama. But I was glued to my spot.

Dad didn't look a speck different from that day Lincoln had first met us in the hayfield. He didn't pay any attention to the woman a'tall.

"Seems you've upgraded your wardrobe," he said.

Lincoln glanced down at the woman. "Yes," he said, "Inheritance brought refinements I failed to achieve on my own.

"I've come all this way to pay the dues I owe, Yarborough. I took your money and wrecked your horse. Now that I've acquired some means, I've brought you enough cash to pay for your trouble, for your good horse, hell, enough to where you can cart your whole family away from this patch a scrub and live in ease." He shook off that woman's arm, took his wallet from his coat, and sure enough, it was stuffed with cash.

You could hear all the hands inhale. I know they wanted to whistle or shout, but we didn't dare make a sound until Dad had his say.

Dad's eyes grazed those bills and then, for the first time he took a good look at that woman with the pink hat.

"I'm sorry for ya, Lincoln," he said, "'cause those refinements you speak of seem to have clouded your vision. All you've got there is a handful of sawdust and ink. A real Lincoln would know that."

Lincoln thumbed those bills and closed his wallet. He

smiled. "As you like, Yarborough," he said. "The Duchess and I have detained you long enough."

And without another word, he stuffed that woman back in the car and folded in behind her. I thought back to the day the Sheriff had driven him off in handcuffs. I guess Lincoln believed he was a bigger feller now.

The driver shut the door on 'em, spun that car around and left us in the dust all over again.

Lawrence took a long sip from his coffee mug and leaned back in his chair. His eyes were blue as snow crystals when the sun strikes them just right.

"Now would I make up something like that?"

His Mild Yoke

Jamie Lisa Forbes

The Widow Smalls and Other Stories

My mother, in my father's hip boots, casts her fishing line. Her hair is the color of cattails, and the breeze that teases the willows lifts it off her neck. I stand on the river bank, eye to eye with the seed tips of the summer grass. Tuffy, our floppy dog, sits next to me. She has a thick reddish coat streaked with black stripes, silky to the touch. She lifts her head to meet my fingers and her tail, matted with burrs, thumps on the ground.

I jump when my mother hooks a fish. The trout whiplashes at the end of the line and the tossed spray sparkles. My mother reels it in, removes the hook and hands it to me. It slithers through my hands and thrashes in the grass. I watch until its flailing subsides and then I run my forefinger down the slimy pink smudge on its belly. It smells of wet moss and rock.

Tuffy looks up at my mother.

My mother calls to my father who strides across the meadow toward the hay stacker half a mile away. She calls several times, each time louder. At last he stops. He points to the stacker and walks on. *Not now*, we understand, *not while there's hay to put up.* He continues on toward the topless slab stack, waiting, like an open box, to be filled with billows of sweet hay.

In the evenings when he comes home, I have to tip my

chin straight up to the ceiling to see his face, but now, against the sprawling meadows and sky, he is a speck in a white tee-shirt and a straw hat.

The tackle bag, heavy with dead fish, droops off my mother's arm.

These are my parents.

Above is our crystal dome of sky. Although nearly everything is larger than me, I know the places and purposes of all things. I know the trees that can be climbed, the gates that can be swung on and the sheds where the calves are born. I know the moon as it withers and bloats across the sky. My world is indestructible.

On hot days when the sun beats down in the yard, I crawl through the flap door in the barn wall and Tuffy follows behind me. She sits and scratches the top of her head with her hind leg before settling on the worn plank floor.

The barn is always cool. It smells of manure and horse hair. Old harnesses line the posts of the stalls. Dust motes sift down through the loft above and the cats skip and play in them. They sit, curl their tails about their feet and stare at me with green eyes. I try to pick them up, but they scatter when I approach, and though I chase after them, I can't find them.

Our hired help, Joyce and Red, live at the bunkhouse. In the mornings, I go with Joyce to milk the cow. We sing *The Farmer in the Dell* as we walk to the milking shed. Joyce pours feed in the bin for Rosie, our cow, and she ambles in without us having to push her. Joyce pulls on Rosie's tits and the milk rings as it hits the bottom of the pail.

"Would you like to try?" she asks.

I sit on the stool and squeeze the velvety tits as hard as I can. Nothing happens.

Joyce laughs. You'll get it one day, honey, when you're bigger. She takes my place and fills the bucket until it is brimming with frothy milk.

After she runs the milk through the separator, I dip

my finger in the mason jar of cream and pop it in my mouth. I glance at Joyce to see if she minds. She yanks my ponytail a little and smiles. She doesn't mind.

Red does not have red hair, but Joyce does. It's in springy curls all over her head. I tell her that I love the color of her hair, and she says, "Thank you, honey, but I color it. "

"With crayons?" I ask.

"Sort of like crayons, honey, but it's liquid," she says.

I try to imagine rows of liquid hair colors arranged in a crayon box.

We bake pies in the kitchen. She ties an apron around me and I sink my hands in the flour and squeeze it through my fingers until it drops in clumps on the wooden board. I roll out the dough slowly so I can savor this motion and the squishy feel of the dough.

While the pies bake, Joyce gives me a glass of milk and a plate of honey grahams. I swing my legs and watch beads of sweat run down the kitchen windows. At noon, my father and Red come in for lunch and I listen to the rise and fall of their voices. I do not grasp all the words, but in the rhythm of their phrases, I hear the knowledge of everything. One day I, too, will speak in phrases like these.

I wake deep in the night and instead of moonlight, I see the light on outside my bedroom. I get up and find my father in his chair, reading. When he reads, he wears thick black-framed glasses. I crawl into his lap and ask him why he is awake, and he answers that it is his only time to read Milton.

I ask why he has to read Milton instead of going to sleep, and he answers that Milton was the greatest poet who ever lived, even though he was blind.

"Everybody should know Milton," he says. "Listen:

...God doth not need
Either man's work or his own gifts; who best
Bear his mild yoke, they serve him best.

His state is kingly.
Thousands at his bidding speed
And post o'er land and ocean without rest....

The words mingle with my dreams. I see creatures with wings, creatures with legs, a multitude so vast they're all a blur, streaming over the globe while I sleep. Come morning, when I open my eyes to the sunshine bouncing off the ponds in the meadow, I know they are out there somewhere.

When the grass blanches in November, a truck and horse trailer come lumbering through our gate. The trailer bounces over the potholes in the driveway. It is my grandfather. There is a pony inside for me.

Everything happens too slowly. My grandfather slides out of the driver's seat. He is shorter than my father, except when he is wearing his cowboy hat, as he is now. He wears a big silver belt buckle with a cowboy on a bronc. He squats down to my height and asks me if I am ready to ride my pony.

I want to see my pony so badly that I nod up and down even though I am also scared.

My mother yanks me away from the back door of the trailer while my father opens it. My grandfather steps inside and murmurs to the pony. The trailer rattles as the pony backs out step by step. Then its hind feet touch the ground and it whirls around.

My grandfather is holding the lead rope. He asks me if I like him.

I do like him. He has sprung from a fairy tale. He is clove-colored with a black mane and tail, white stocking feet and a white diamond on his forehead. He paws the ground and jerks the lead rope. It is because he is eager to be with me, I think.

My father saddles the pony and then I am lifted onto him. My mother curls my fingers around the reins. She steps back to take pictures. I smile, but under me I sense seething muscle and will.

I set off with my father and grandfather on their leggy sorrels. They are ahead of me and the pony trots to catch up, but then they trot, too, and so the pony runs. At first, the feeling of catapulting through space makes me giggle. Then giddiness turns to terror when I realize I can't stop. I want to get off. I let go of the reins. I let go of the saddle horn and then I am tumbling and the ground rises up and I bounce and roll. I am stunned by the hard smack of earth.

My father and grandfather stop and look back. The pony stands over me. I sob. He should be sorry, that's what I think, but he regards me as if I was no more than a mosquito. He shifts from foot to foot.

My grandfather trots back and gets off his horse. He does not try to lift me off the ground.

"Why did you let go?" he asks.

I look at his lined face, his crossed arms. The answer — that I was scared — is the wrong answer, so I sob even harder.

"Cowgirls do not bawl when they fall off their horses," he says.

My father comes and wipes my face with his handkerchief.

"You must ride your pony," my grandfather says, "or I will sell it to some other little girl."

I want the pony so I stop crying and nod. My father sets me back in the saddle. I want to ride, I want to be as good a rider as that cowboy on my grandfather's belt buckle, but instead, I cling to the saddle horn the whole way home.

In the barnyard, my father says to my grandfather, "She'll do better next time."

I never do better. And so, one day, when I am not looking, the pony goes away.

Ring-ring-ring. Our telephone ring is three rings, followed by a pause. Ring-ring-ring. I am drifting back to sleep, but the house is awake. Lights snap on. My parents are whispering in the hall, their voices tense and urgent. I slip out of bed and find my mother in the kitchen standing at the window.

Go back to sleep, she says, but the tone underneath her words says, something is happening.

"Where's Daddy?"

"He's gone to fight the fire," she says. "The barn is burning down."

"Can I see?" I ask.

"No, go back to bed."

I go back to the living room and climb on my father's reading chair. Now I can see out the window.

It's not the barn that's burning. It's the whole sky. Orange flames consume it. Between our house and the barn, everything is tinged with orange: the skeletons of cottonwoods, outbuildings, trucks. There is a line of men standing outside the ring of trucks, and I cannot see whether my father is among them or not.

In the morning, my mother and I go out to look at what remains. Tuffy follows us, sniffing at the air. I am shocked that in just a night, the barn is gone. The roof has collapsed and the charred beams are smoldering. A skiff of snow coats the debris.

Where are the cats who used to play on the floor?

My father is on the bulldozer, smashing everything into one pile. In a few days, there is nothing left of the barn except the scorched ground. After that, as the snow mounds higher and higher, I am comforted that the fire is smothered beneath the drifts.

The Widow Smalls and Other Stories

At Christmas time, we go to the schoolhouse for the neighborhood party. All our neighbors are there, the men with their reddened faces and the women with their callused hands. There is a big Santa Claus who hands out gifts to the children, and I open mine to find a painted blue box with a big red heart in the middle.

"You can put treats inside," says Santa, "for your pony."

I will save treats for the pony who might return one day.

My father stands me in the front of the room and tells me to recite my poem. Behind me is the blackboard and the chalk dust sifts up my nose. I look out over the people leaning forward in their chairs.

> When I consider how my light is spent
> Ere half my days, in this dark world, and wide,
> And that one talent, which is death to hide,
> Lodged with me...

I struggle with the next word because in all our practicing, I have said, yush-less.

> use-less. . .

I sigh with relief. This room is warm. The people are all smiling. I can feel them holding their breath with expectation. And with great drama, I raise my voice to launch into the last line:

> They also serve who only Stand-and-Wait!

Everyone claps when I finish. I am startled by the sound and amazed by the power of Milton.

As I start toward my parents, a man in the front row with crinkly eyes grips my arm and says, "Honey, what's that poem about?

"God will come if we wait," I answer.

I am riding my tricycle round and round our yard one morning when, to my surprise, my father comes home. He never comes home during the day. The frost is out of the ground now and the air is heavy with the odor of damp earth. My father does not speak to me. He goes in the house and then leaves without even looking at me. Something is wrong.

I go inside and my mother is sitting at the table, sobbing. "Tuffy is dead," she says.

I do not understand this, so I continue to stand, waiting for meaning.

My father had gone to see our neighbors, she said, the neighbors who raise sheep. Tuffy jumped out of the truck when he wasn't looking and triggered a cyanide bomb. A cyanide bomb used for killing the coyotes.

Cy-a-nide. I roll this word round and round on my tongue. It is a hard word to say.

"Get out," my mother says. "Get out, go outside."

I do not move.

"Get out!" she screams.

Back outside, I crawl onto the burlap bed in Tuffy's house. The space smells like her and I cannot understand how she can be gone when her smell is so alive. I look out the opening, mesmerized by this hole rent in our lives.

I walk down to Joyce's and tell her what has happened. Joyce has a sewing machine and scraps of cloth on a large table. She lets me pick the scraps I like and helps me hand-sew them together.

"You can make a quilt for your mother," she says. "That will make her feel better."

This seems wonderful. I know my mother will be happy to have a quilt from me, and I work eagerly on my squares. Lunchtime comes, the men come in and Joyce tells me I can work on it some more tomorrow.

I never see it again.

The Widow Smalls and Other Stories

When the dandelions pop and the leaves unfurl, Joyce and Red leave. I watch them as they load their belongings onto a horse trailer.

Joyce hugs me goodbye.

"When will you be back?" I ask.

She pats my shoulder and smiles.

"I don't know."

She waves as she climbs into the truck and then they drive away. They stop to open the gate and then they pull out on the county road and their truck speeds away. The sound breaks apart and dissipates until it's gone.

Still, I listen. I hear frogs in the meadow and a collage of birdsong in the trees. Joyce and Red have left the gate open. It swings in the breeze and I hear it creak. Our cattle brand is welded on top of it. Beyond that gate is the world where the thousands speed and post without rest. Joyce and Red have joined them.

I listen. I want to hear the thud and roar of that world, but I cannot hear anything.

I stare at the empty space where the gate should rest. I am waiting for it to close.

Jamie Lisa Forbes

Crack-The-Whip

Jamie Lisa Forbes

The Widow Smalls and Other Stories

When I turned in the driveway, Lord a' mighty, the house was a'blazing like the Star of Bethelem! It ain't been like that in a long time. Most nights now only the kitchen light's on. I slid out of the truck, studying the spectacle. Commotion leaked from the walls like I ain't heard in years: laughter and chatter and baby squeals.

Up above, no stars in the heavens. Maybe snow tomorra.

My hand shook as I lit my cigarette, and not just 'cause I'm an old Jack Mormon. Ally's Beetle was in the driveway. My baby girl'd come home! It's been over a year! Who knows, maybe she's ready to quit that Denver nonsense and come home for good.

She opened the door. Just to look at her—I couldn't stop grinning. She was lovelier than ever with those broad, strong shoulders and that tawny mane falling to her waist. That spark in her green eyes—for me, I thought. Then it sputtered.

"The prodigal daughter," I cried, "home from the dens of sin!"

She tried to dredge up a smile but I thought she was gonna close the door.

"It's you, Daddy. I thought you were Kit."

"What if I ain't? Doesn't a daughter have a hug and a kiss for her father?"

She trod down those steps like her feet were made a lead. A year away hadn't improved her none. I run smack into that same wall a spite in her eyes. She glanced down at my cigarette.

"You know I can't give up these things," I said.

"I remember when you made Kit spend a night in the garage for smoking."

"You ain't seen me in a year and that's all ya got to say?"

Her face softened up some—we both know her faith's taught her better than that—and she raised up and pecked me on the cheek.

"Happy Thanksgiving, Daddy."

Then she fled. *Kit's the damn bishop at his ward. Don't I get the credit for that?*

I ground out the cigarette in the dirt.

Tessie met me at the door with her toddler perched on her hip.

"How's that little orangutan today?"

"Stop it, Daddy."

"Them bug eyes and them orange hairs sticking out of her head. What do you think she looks like? Where'd Ally go? I want to talk to her."

"That's it. You're through with us. The rest of us are nothin' compared to her. Go say hi to Mick."

Mick and Brigham—Bing, as we call him—were arm-wrestling at the card table. I don't care if Mick is Tessie's dreamboat, he's got hair too long for me. I know Jesus wore his hair that way, but with all the miracles he had to work on the wretched hordes, he didn't have no time to run to the barber shop.

"Mick, what are you picking on the boy for?"

"Just a friendly game, Paul."

"Well, next time, pick on somebody your own size."

Bing's my youngest, about to finish high school. Just in the last year, he's shot up tall as an aspen. Mighty odd to have to look up at your own son. Of all of 'em, he's been the least trouble, always quiet, always minded Mother and me. When I watch him strut out the door in the morning, tossing his hair off his forehead, I think, God, that's the young man I woulda liked to have been. Carefree. All the world ahead of him.

"Happy Thanksgiving, Father." That was my daughter-in-law, Beth. She beamed with pride, holding little Samuel in her arms.

"Well, lookee here. Can I hold him?"

She passed him off to me, and the weight of his head sank into the crook of my arm. I switched my hand around to the back of his neck. He frowned hard to focus on my face. Four of these creatures once were mine. I've looked into their eyes and tried just as hard to read them as they tried to read me.

Thud. Brigham's arm hit the card table. I rolled the baby back into Beth's arms.

"All right, all right, up off the chair, Bing, and I'll show you how to take care of your brother-in-law."

"It's Thanksgiving," said Mick. "Let's give it a rest."

"No, boy, you come on. You've been pickin' on the yearling here. Let's see you take on the old bull."

"I don't want to."

I set my elbow on the table. Tessie fluttered over like a hen.

"Daddy, he says he doesn't want to. Why don't you let him alone?"

"Waitin' on you, Mick."

Mick got up.

"Ah—ah! You see there, Bing, the merest glimpse of might sends him scurrying."

"Don't you get it, Paul? I don't want to!"

"When then? You give me the time and place."

Roly-poly Mother popped out of the kitchen.

"Dinner's ready. Paul, better wash up."

I don't know what's gotten into Mother. With them coon

rings around her eyes, she always looks well...old. I ain't no spring chicken. My hair's as sparse and gray as hers. But I'm rarin' to greet each new day. The joy of life has dribbled outta her. I don't understand it.

She and Ally ferried platters to the table, and when they were done, I hoisted the turkey in. The tribe settled in their seats, all eyes on me. I let the pause hold a little to bump them into a solemn mood.

"Heavenly Father, we are so very grateful for Your Thanksgiving Day with our Ally just come home from the big city of Denver where only You know why she had to go, but we trusted You'd watch over her and bring her home safe and here she is—home."

Baby Samuel squalled, ruining my blessing.

"Beth, damn it, get that baby outta here!" She jumped up and left the table. The rest of 'em fidgeted, then they squared their shoulders and quieted, waiting for me to go on.

Just when I'd taken a breath to dive back into it, Ally murmured, "She kept him up so you could see him when you came in."

"Honey, I already seen him when I come in the door. Now I gotta start all over..."

The front door opened. "Hello?"

"Kit!" Ally squealed and flew to him with the rest of them trailing behind. When I got there, she was squeezing the life out of her older brother. Him—not me.

"Samuel's beautiful!"

"We missed you when he was born."

"I'm sorry I wasn't here."

He held her by the shoulders. "Are you happy down there, Ally?"

I listened hard. I wanted to know the answer to that one.

She pulled away from him and her chin dropped. That told me all I needed to know.

"I'm happy, but I miss everyone."

"You're the first one of us to go that far from home."

She laughed. "You talk like it's the other side of the world. It's only six hours away."

Way before all these kids was born, I heard the call of the wide world. I guess that's the part of me that's in her. You bet—she's got drive to be able to take off on her own like that. The rest of 'em here, they ain't never going to have it.

But it ain't what she's 'sposed to do. She's 'sposed to be home starting a family, like Tessie and Beth.

I cut in. "How's the bean-counter?" I said.

If those emerald flecks in Ally's eyes had been spears, I'd a been skewered. "Bean-counter?"

Tessie jumped in. "He's been calling Kit that ever since K-Mart promoted him to store manager."

She beamed at him. "You got promoted? That's wonderful! I'm so proud."

The way the hall light was bouncing off his pate, it hit me—Kit's losing his hair! Plus he hadn't shaved. His clothes look like he slept at that store last night. He put his arm over Ally's shoulder and looked at all of us.

"Where's Beth?" he asked.

Everyone stared at me.

"I believe she's nursin' the baby," I said. "The child fussed just as I was starting grace."

Kit nodded. He knows his old man.

"Maybe with you here now, Daddy will wait for Beth," said Ally.

"No, we ain't standing here all night. Mother's food is getting cold, and there's no telling how long it'll take for that child to nurse."

"No one minds waiting for Kit and Beth," she said.

"You wait for 'em then! And while you're all standing here, maybe you'll think on your father, a working man, ready for his hot meal. Look at Kit! He's happy to let his old dad go on and eat supper in peace."

Kit touched Ally's arm.

"It's OK, Ally, go on and sit down. We'll be along."

"I want you with us."

"We'll have plenty of time together, Ally. I promise."

When they'd settled back in their places, I picked up where I'd left off.

"For all these blessings, O Heavenly Father, we are eternally grateful, and as we sit here under this roof, may we be ever mindful of Thy Roof that shelters us all, in the name of Your Son, Our Savior, Jesus Christ…"

"Amen," said everyone, and Mother began passing the serving dishes.

"You're coming home for Bing's graduation, aren't you, Ally?" asked Mother.

"Sure am." She shot a glance across the table at her younger brother. "What are you doing after graduation, Bing?"

The boy's mouth was already so full of stuffing that nobody understood what he said.

"Speak up," I said. "Tell 'er your good news."

Bing cleared his throat. "I'm going to work with Dad."

She looked back at me. She kept her trap shut, but that old stony defiance was there in her eyes. I've seen it many a time. It always made me want to raise a hand to her.

"Don't you bother him," I said, "Bing knows the work. And, unlike the wayward lamb I might mention, he wants to stay put with his family. It's a good living, best possible start for a young man like him."

"That's the best possible start for you, Bing?" she asked.

Bing glanced at me, his mouth still full of food. "Dad says I'll be making $30.00 an hour by the time I'm twenty."

"What other choices did you have?"

"Well, he's rejected the dropping-outta-school-and-running-off-to-Denver option," I said. Score one for the old man—her eyes dropped to her plate!

"Daddy," said Tessie, "has Ally told you? She's been promoted, too. She's the manager at the dry-cleaning store."

Mother looked up from passing the sweet potatoes. "Ally! I hadn't heard that."

Ally shrugged. "It's nothing. It's not like Kit."

"Maybe now that you've got some experience, you could move back home, manage old Sandy's dry cleaners downtown," I said.

You'd think I'd shattered a glass the way the room got so quiet — and frosty.

"I'm not coming home, Daddy."

So it's not the prodigal daughter returning after all. I shoulda realized the moment I saw her at the door.

"I'm sorry to hear that, daughter. You don't begin to know how sorry I feel."

If anything, the temperature in the room dipped another few degrees.

"You were tired of us. You were charmed by temptations that beckoned you, I guess. If you've thrown aside your faith, that's where you belong. But you lied out there to Kit just now. You ain't happy. You can't be. And if the best you've been able to do for yourself is working at a dry cleaner's, I don't understand why that dirty old city is such a better place than here."

Her voice cracked a little. "I haven't fallen out of the faith. Denver's my home. I like it there. It's where I live."

"You got something goin' on there, a boy or something, or you'd come home." I reached for the rolls. "Are you going to church?"

She stared back at me. "No."

I started to grunt a little but then Mick had to pitch his two cents in.

"Ally, you oughtta save some money and travel around, you know, go see other places."

"Look who's yakking," I said, "You been in school for

five years, you still ain't got an income, your family practically lives here, and you're giving advice."

"You want her to spend her life at the dry cleaner's?"

"No, damn it, that's what I've been trying to say for the last thirty minutes. Ally, you've been gone a year, but that mountain a pride still keeps you from listening to me."

She put her hands in her lap. "I hear you all the time, Daddy."

I leaned back in my chair. "Everything I've done, I done for all of you. I never had the chance to take off and go anywhere! I had brothers and sisters to feed. Every one of you sitting at this table has gotten better than what I got."

They all got up. Mother, too. She set a slice of pumpkin pie in front of me as she left.

I read the sky right. It snowed on Friday. Saturday morning, frost patches covered the windows and the world sparkled. Everyone was clamoring to get out on the ice rink, Tessie, too, so Mother agreed to watch her baby.

Ally went to the phone to invite Kit and Beth. I told her it was a waste of time. I watched her face while he droned on about how he couldn't leave his bean-counting, blah, blah, blah. The boy's changed—now that he's a pillar of the community. He can't divvy out a slice of time to this family anymore. With every word from him, her voice dropped lower. 'Bout time she found out what it's like when a loved one don't measure up.

By the time we got there, the sun was high and bright colors spun round the rink like flakes in a kaleidoscope. Bing found his clan, a bunch of rangy boys like him, and they skated round the outer edge. Mick and Tessie skated together, holding hands. And Ally was everywhere. The old Ally was back, the fairy-child who could make a stump smile. She talked and laughed with everyone. Everyone recognized her.

Everyone was glad to see her. They flocked to her like honeybees to clover. Everyone wanted a snatch of her.

I watched all of 'em from the warmin' hut. My children. All growed now. When they was little, we'd come out to this rink and play crack-the-whip. Their little faces would sparkle with excitement and I'd tell 'em to hang on and I'd lead 'em in a big snake trail while they giggled until I'd crack a sharp turn and send one or two of them flying. Oh, how they'd laugh!

Kit did get his arm broke one time.

I put on my skates and went out into the snappy air. I worked up some speed, came up behind Tessie and Mick and jerked her away from him.

"Daddy!" she hollered. "What are you doing?"

"Stealing you away for a minute or two. You don't mind five minutes with your old dad, do you?"

"You're hurting my arm." She turned to look over her shoulder. "Where's Mick?" Then she caught an edge and fell.

"Sorry, honey," I said as I held out a hand to help her up.

Mick skated up. "What are you doing, Paul?"

"Nothing. It's just a little accident is all."

"You know what, Paul?" he said. His face was red and bloated. "They hate you, do you know that? All of 'em. Kit, Ally, Tess, Bing. All of 'em."

"What the heck's gotten into you, son?"

He stood there, fuming, and I shoved him. Damned if he didn't shove back. I lost my balance and fell hard on my shoulder.

Ally skated up. Mick backed away quick, like he was scared of me, the little runt, as he shoulda been. I wanted to get up and beat the crap out of him, but I'd lost my wind.

Ally squatted next to me. "Are you all right?"

"I'm all right."

"I'll help you up."

"No, damn it, I can handle myself. Just leave me be."

She backed off to where Mick and Tessie stood. I hauled

myself to my feet and the three of 'em looked at me like I'd grown horns. I bent over a second until I could breathe again.

"Maybe you're right, Mick. Maybe Kit and Ally and your wife all hate me. But you know what? It don't hurt me none. It's going to hurt every one of them as they try to live with themselves all the years to come."

I shifted to look at Ally. How those eyes shone. I had her attention this time all right.

"But you're wrong about Bing. He's the one, the only one of 'em, who looks up at me as a child should — I know that."

That night Mother fixed ham and scalloped potatoes for supper. It was quiet, not the quiet after a happy day out in the fresh air, but quiet like someone was about to tell me something I didn't want to hear.

Ally spoke up. Her cheeks were all rosy from the skating rink.

"I won't be home for Christmas."

"You'll be missed." I said it as flat as I could. No point anymore in showing her how mad or sad I was.

Silence again.

"After graduation, Bing's coming with me."

I looked over to him. He dropped his head and his hair fell in his eyes.

"Is that true?"

He glanced at Ally and nodded.

"I sure would like to know what's in this town of Denver that's such a draw. What are you traipsing off for?"

"He'll be starting community college," said Ally.

"And, in Denver, it's free?"

Now the pup yapped. "Ally says there's plenty of work. She'll help me find a job."

I turned to her. "You talked him into this, didn't you?"

Unlike Bing's, her eyes met me head on. "Yes."

"He has a job, you know. Right here. Working for H-G Excavating."

"I've been thinking Dad, before Ally came home," Bing said. "I don't know if that's what I want for the rest of my life. You've always said you want me to have a better life."

"What are you listening to her for? Stay here. There's a community college here."

"Then he'd have to live with you and he doesn't want that."

"Can the boy speak for himself, Ally?"

Bing jumped to his feet. It startled me so to see him standing over me. I didn't recognize him.

"You go on and on about how, when you went to work, it was all over for you! Have you ever thought about what I think when you say that, how scared that makes me that I'd turn out like you?"

"What about your old man? You'd up and leave, after all that's been done for you?"

Everyone had stopped eating. Mother sat with her hands in her lap and her head bowed.

"What does this have to do with you, Daddy?" Ally said.

"A man wants his sons beside him, like Abraham and Issac! You don't have to take my boy! Bing's got nothing to do with what's between you and me."

"Aren't you listening?" shouted Bing. "I want to go!"

I looked from Ally to Bing. She'd bewitched him all right. But there was no undoing it.

"I've got to get some fresh air." I pushed away from the table and stomped outside.

My heart was thumping against my ribcage and my skull felt like it was 'bout to burst. I lit a cigarette to calm down. All the house lights were on in the neighborhood. Everyone home—with their families. What was it like behind those other walls? Were their holiday suppers like this?

Other children love their parents, that's what I think. There's old Grafton Wheeler's house. His kid's going on a mission to China. And Jimmy Saxon's house. His kids all work in the bakery with him. When I see my neighbors in church, these boys and girls sit shoulder to shoulder with their parents, looking straight ahead, their faces aglow. How come I'm the only one plumb out in the dark?

Next morning, the alarm rang at four and I got up. My shift starts at five. I pulled on my union suit and a pair of jeans and headed for the kitchen. The light was on and dammed if Ally wasn't parked there at the table!

"What are you doing up?"

"I couldn't sleep." Her voice was softer, it didn't have that battle edge to it.

"You want some cocoa?" She didn't have to answer. I knew she did. I set the pot on the stove. "How come you couldn't sleep?"

"At the skating rink...what you said...you're right. Hating you never stops hurting, it doesn't matter where I am."

I turned to look at her and leaned back against the stove. "It's not stopping you from taking Bing away from me."

She wiped a tear away. "That was about Bing. Not you."

"Well, I see Bing's a grown man. He can do what he wants. But you could have warned me first, girl. You didn't have to hit me over the head with it."

"You would have tried to stop me."

I sat at the table with her and we drank our cocoa, not speaking.

When I got my coat on, she said, "I'll sit with you 'till the truck warms up."

"What for?"

"Because it'll be another half a year 'til I see you again."

The snow crunched underneath our feet and the cold bit hard. But the sky was such a wonder that a man could have watched it 'till he froze to death. Heaven must look as vast as that sky. And as cold. And each angel must be as bright and silent as those stars. Or maybe they sing at a pitch we can't hear.

I got the truck started. Ally's hair shone under the dome light. I lit up a cigarette and she cranked down the window, letting all that icy air in.

"You're going to kill me, Ally."

"You're killing yourself."

"God's not worrying about my smoking. He knows what's in my heart." The smoke spiraled out towards those stars. I took another long draw. "Listen, you tell Bing I'll pay for his tuition."

"That'll mean a lot to him."

The seconds ticked by 'till she spoke again. "Daddy, I've gone back to school. I'm going to finish high school. Then, next fall, I want to start college."

I nearly dropped the cigarette. "Well, I'll be damned Ally! I might not always agree with you, but you make me sit up and take notice. I always wanted you to stay in school. You remember what I said about it, don't you? But old hard-headed you. Nothing could keep you there after you turned sixteen."

"You didn't want me to succeed in school. You did everything to make sure I'd fail."

"What are you talking about?"

Now those tears I'd seen earlier were near choking her.

"I could never do anything right. That's all I ever heard from you."

"I wanted you to help your mother and to help out with Tessie and Bing. But that look in your eyes, Ally, you've always resisted me."

I reached in my pocket and passed her a handkerchief.

"It don't much matter now, I guess. It's so far past it

don't seem like I ever raised any of you at all. But if you're determined to go ahead, Ally, I want you to know I'm behind you. And I'll help you pay for it."

She shifted, and O Lord, thank you, all that spite dropped right out of those eyes! I looked in 'em—and saw me. All my own dreams and longings, most of 'em long gone. Looking at Ally has always been like looking in the mirror. When she was a child, I'd look in those eyes and see weakness. And because it was my weakness, I'd get the belt and try to thrash it out of her.

Now, sitting across from me, I think she was seeing herself in me—for the first time ever. I watched the thought ripple through her 'til it was gone. She wouldn't let herself believe it.

She kissed me on the cheek.

"Be careful, Daddy," she said, and she got out of the truck. I watched her walk back to the house. She turned into a shadow, then—dark. And I got that odd feeling I get when a trench caves in and a man goes under. That if you could touch time, if you could just reach back to the last wavering second and give it a tug, you could pull him free.

Or pull your child back and hold her until she says, "I love you, Daddy." But you stand there and the seconds fly away from you. You might as well try and grab a flock of sparrows. They're gone in less than a thought. Someone else has been playing crack-the-whip and it wasn't like what you thought, you weren't at the lead, all along you were at the tail end.

The Good War

Jamie Lisa Forbes

The Widow Smalls and Other Stories

I

"**Damn you, Rosie!** Damn your worthless hide!"
Cal yanked the mare's head around and booted her
flank. She wouldn't stand against the outhouse like he wanted
her to! It was his own fault! If he'd woken up earlier and grained
her, she wouldn't be so determined to get back to the barn. All
she had to do was stand — dammit — for ten seconds, so he could
climb that roof before Jean got out.

There. Rosie's head drooped. Either she understood what
he wanted, or she was too lazy to fight anymore. He dropped
the reins, pulled up his feet and slowly stood, teetering on her
broad back as he reached out for the overhang. She moved and
he lunged, only to miss and fall in the snow. *Damn, damn, damn.*

As he shook the snow off, clumps slipped down his
collar, melting in icy streaks down his back. Rosie dozed, vapor
from her nostrils barely visible in the gray light.

Two more attempts, then Cal heaved himself onto the

roof. *Quiet!* He held his breath and listened for some squawk below that would tell him he'd been discovered. It'd be a miracle if Jean hadn't heard anything, what with all the tromping around Rosie had done.

Slowly, he exhaled. Nothing. He scooted over and reached for the bucket of snow he'd hung on a nail. The sky paled above the pines. He curled his fingers and blew into them. What the heck was she doing in there anyway? He could have crapped ten times by now. He was starting to shiver when at last the door hinge screeched, and as she stepped out, he up-ended the bucket of snow on her head.

Oh, the blood-curdling scream! Cal looked up through the pines — and smiled.

Then, "Cal! You get down here! Cal!"

He curled into a ball and soon she stomped away down the snow-shoveled path.

Tickled with his success, Cal jumped down and collected Rosie. He led her to the barn and filled up her grain box and Hank's. The darkness had lifted, bringing back the day-time barn with its worn saddles and horse collars. He leaned against the stall post. The sound of heavy jaws cracking the oat husks added to Cal's general good feelings.

As he stepped out, a ping whizzed past his ear and whacked the side of the barn. Jean stood on the front porch aiming the BB gun dead at him. He dove into the snow.

"Jean!" Snow sprayed his face. "You're going to hit my eye!"

"Say you're sorry!"

"For what?"

A pellet hit his shoulder. "Ow! Jean! I'm not going to saddle your horse!"

"Jean, what the heck!" His dad's voice. *Saved.*

"He dumped snow on me coming out of the outhouse!"

Cal leaped to his feet. "I didn't. A gust came along and blew it down! I saw it."

His father glared at him—then at Jean.

"Three straight weeks of snow, your mother's near to losing her mind, but the two of you just go on and on. Get in here for breakfast."

Cal dropped his chin to hide his smirk. He stopped on the porch and yanked off his overshoes. Gus, their border collie, thumped his tail against the floor. He stroked the dog's head and listened to the sounds inside: bacon frying, a chair dragging on the floor, Jean whining.

At the stove, his mother whipped milk gravy round and round. Wisps of ash-colored hair spilled over her forehead. Last summer, he'd passed her in height, but when her face stiffened—like it did now—he was afraid of her.

"Sit down, Charles Christian."

As soon as he'd scooted his chair up to the table, Jean kicked him in the shin.

"Ow!"

The whisk clattered against the pan. "Frank! Get him out of here!" His mother's voice was shrill as a hen's.

His father put his arm around her and steered her away from the stove.

"It's all right, Edie. I'll take care of it. Why don't you go back to the bedroom?"

"Breakfast, Frank."

"I'll take care of it."

The bedroom door shut and Cal looked into Jean's face.

"See what you did," she hissed.

"I don't know what you're talking about."

"I better not hear a sound out there!" Dad's voice boomed from the bedroom.

Cal was on his second helping of bacon, eggs, biscuits and milk gravy before his father came back out. He sat down heavily at the table.

"Your mama's got a splitting headache. You two won't be happy 'til you kill her."

"I didn't do anything," Cal said. He gestured toward his sister. "Jean's gone stir-crazy with all the snow."

"Uh-uh," said Dad without looking up. "The bucket in front of the outhouse says she's not."

Cal inwardly cursed the detail he'd overlooked.

Dad sopped up the rest of his gravy with a biscuit.

"You need to tailor your opinion of yourself a tad, don't you think?"

Jean swept up the dishes while Cal dressed to go back outside. Sunbeams poked through the pines, catching the snow crystals sifting from the boughs. Cal shoveled the path to the chicken hut and saddled Jean's horse so she could ride to school. He couldn't leave until feeding was done.

Cal and his father harnessed the horses to the sled. With the sled empty, Rosie and Hank trotted out, fired by the grain in their bellies. They tossed their manes and divets of snow flew up behind their hooves. Cal watched the house and barn recede behind them. There came Gus, running in their tracks.

Cal opened the barbed wire gate to the stackyard and his father drove through. The horses pulled up next to the hay and Cal climbed up and pitched.

His father cupped his hands to his mouth and sang out, "Commmmm up, you ladies. Commmmm up, you gals. Heyyyy, dollies!"

His voice reverberated across the meadow and cows bawled responses. They struck out through the snow trails.

"Commmm up here, you gals."

The younger ones stampeded and soon a crowd milled at the open gate, policed by Gus. He scurried from side to side, barring them from charging in.

"Got a count on 'em yet, Charles Christian?"

The daily count irritated Cal as much as his birth name. His count was never right. "Eighty-two," he muttered.

"Wrong. Ninety-six. They're all here."

How could Dad count and make all that noise at the same time?

His father beamed, as if he'd read Cal's mind. "Someday, Charles Christian, with a little more practice, you'll get it."

He said that every day.

They pulled out of the stackyard with the cows trailing behind. His father let the horses pull by themselves and the two of them pitched. Cal pitched as fast as he could to finish his side first, but if his father knew a contest was on, he was ignoring it.

He sang. *Buffalo gals, won't you come out tonight, come out tonight, come out tonight. Buffalo gals, won't you come out tonight and dance by the light of the moon.*

"Dad, I'm done."

His father turned around. "Well, so you are. You can do the work of three men, son. Did you spot any early calvers?"

"No, but that one's got a bad eye."

His father peered at the one he'd pointed out. "Good catch. I'll ride back out here and get her."

"I want to do it."

"You've got to get to school."

"Please?"

"No, that teacher of yours gives me what-for as it is. You fetch water for Mama and then you're going to school."

He could rope that old cow faster than his dad. He imagined riding Spunky—their fastest horse—plunging through the snow with his loop twirling over his head and Spunky's ears laid back, ready to chew on that cow if he had to.

His father let him off at the house.

He brought his mother two buckets of ice that he crushed from blocks stored in the icehouse. He poured one in a basin and set it on the stove. The smell of fresh baked bread filled the kitchen.

"Now you'll help me bring in the wash," she said.

That isn't the kind of work cowhands do. "I'm late for school."

Her eyes bored through him.

"Your father leaves me alone here all day. Spending a few minutes with me is the least you could do. Then I'm going to school with you."

"Why?"

"What with the weather, I haven't been out of here in days and days. I'd just like to get out and breathe, Charles Christian, if it's not too much trouble for you."

He pictured them riding up to the schoolhouse together with everyone gawking out the window.

"How will I get home, then?"

"You can ride back home with Jean."

The sister who was shooting at him this morning. *Better to walk.*

His mother looked in the small mirror as she carefully folded her hair into a scarf. He couldn't understand it. Why did she look in the mirror—like she was dressing up—just to go out and collect laundry? She always did that.

Cal carried the laundry basket while she picked her way through the icy track, her arms wrapped around herself. She squinted against the glare on the snow. The clothes on the line were frozen hard as boards—his father's shirts and pants, his own shirts, Jean's underwear and bras. He tried to skip these last items. He looked pleadingly at his mother.

"What's got into you?" she snapped.

"Nothing." He held the underthings out at arm's length and dropped them in the basket.

When he'd saddled the horse and led it around to the

house, she was waiting at the kitchen table, still wrapped in her coat and scarf. She'd added lipstick, he noticed.

"Do you want to ride in front or back?" he asked.

"Back of you is all right."

He helped her up behind the saddle. Once he'd mounted, she gently wrapped her arms around him.

"Don't jog," she said. "It'll blow my scarf off."

"You'll freeze if we have to walk the whole way."

"I'll be all right. Just don't let him run."

He eased the horse down through the pines. As they broke from the tree cover, the wind smacked them. It was raw on Cal's cheeks, but his mother didn't complain. She was sheltered against him.

"Look, Cal," she said.

He turned his head. Elk browsed in the sage. They were so still, he could barely pick them out. Only a few looked up.

"They're hungry, too hungry to be scared," she said.

If they were still hanging around tomorrow, he might slip down and shoot one.

The gusts strengthened, kicking sheets of snow into his face.

"Mama, can't we go faster?"

"We're almost there now, aren't we?"

He squinted at the schoolhouse below them in the valley. Another mile to go. He switched hands on the reins and balled up the fingers of his free hand in his glove.

The students — Jean included — were outside when they rode up. Cal squirmed as they turned to watch him. Their chatter subsided.

Jean shouted, "What took you so long?"

Plucking your underthings off the damn clothesline. "I had to feed!"

The look on Jean's face was as easy to read as lettering on a blackboard. She didn't want their mother there any more than he did. Had she spoken up, she might have been able to disguise her feelings, but her mule-sized brain had no ability to learn social know-how. She let her feelings show to the whole world, too dumb to understand that was how he and everyone else could get the best of her. In the silence she kept as Mama slid off the horse, she might as well've shouted throughout the schoolyard how embarrassed she was that her mother was there.

"Is that all right with you, Jean Marie, if I come visit your school?" Mama spoke brightly enough, but there was an edge to her voice that made Jean stiffen.

"Mrs. Lansing, how nice of you to come," said Mrs. Jeffries. His mother smiled, reached out and grasped the teacher's hands. Mrs. Jeffries looked startled by the gesture. Cal glanced around to see if any of the others were smirking and sure enough, a few of them were.

"I'm so sorry Cal's late. We needed his help this morning." Mama clung to Mrs. Jeffries' hands as if they were the rope keeping her from drowning. Mrs. Jeffries tried to pull back and then surrendered.

"I understand you and Frank need him, but he's a clever boy and he could be doing so much more if he were here on time."

"He'll catch up, I'm sure. Jeanie will help him."

Cal looked over at her. She stuck her tongue out and the others snickered.

Mrs. Jeffries called them inside. He thought his mother would leave then, but she followed them in.

"Cal, I have something for you." She pulled a brown paper package out of her coat.

He tore it open to find half the loaf of bread she'd made plus homemade cheese.

The bread was soft and chewy and he devoured it whole while Mrs. Jeffries read to them about how the Goths sacked Rome, and his mother rode away, her head bent and the bottom of her scarf whipping in the wind.

II

Nine months later, they lost it all.

The trouble started one evening after Cal and his father had come in from the hayfields, wrung out from the August sun. Cal had just dunked his head in the outdoor tub when the banker drove into the yard.

He didn't think anything of it at first. The banker drove up from Walden every six months or so, but when Dad joked, "Bill, you're always just in time for a meal," the man froze, hands on his hips. Cal felt it then, the first tremor underneath his feet.

Dad didn't seem to feel it. He pestered the man until he'd surrendered at their picnic table in front of a plate piled high with pot roast, carrots, mashed potatoes and a glass of buttermilk. Cal felt that he'd been wrong, that he'd misunderstood — until the banker picked up his fork and set it back down.

"I guess you know why I'm here, Frank."

Dad looked surprised. "No, not quite."

"You're behind."

"Oh, I know that," said Dad, "but I have a good calf crop and I'm expecting to make it up this fall, that is — if cattle prices will pick up. You know I don't have any control over that!"

"Thing is," the man's gaze drifted to the evening star, "the directors have decided to foreclose."

Cal looked to Jean for a clue, but her eyes darted from one parent's face to the other's. Mama put her hands in her lap and for the longest time, the mourning doves' calls filled the space around them until Dad picked up his fork again and gestured to the banker. "You best eat up before it gets cold."

The auction was set for the fall, after haying. On a crisp morning, while the dew shimmered on the aftermath, cars and trucks poured into the yard, unloading the neighbors to pick over all the Lansings owned. Tack and tools and livestock — they poked and prodded as if these things no longer belonged to the family. Cal wanted to stop them, but instead he watched in dumb horror as Dad shook their hands and ferried the women's covered plates to the picnic table where Mama had taken refuge under a wide-brimmed straw hat.

Cal found Jean reading a book in the hayloft.

"There's a bunch of kids chasing your ducks." With any luck, she'd tear outside and act so hideous, she'd scare all the people away.

She turned a page. "Don't matter. They're not ours any more."

"Aren't you going to come down?"

"Not 'till I have to."

"Suit yourself," Cal snapped.

She mocked him, "Suit yourself."

Cal climbed back down and trailed Dad as he advertised their belongings. He pried open Rosie's and Hank's mouths so the men could age them for themselves. He sorted through the rest of the horses, picking out one that each would like.

"See this palomino — Spunky, we call him — best roping horse we've got. He'll be all over a cow before you've got your loop out." Cal grabbed his arm.

"What's the matter, son?"

"Don't let 'em have Spunky!"

"We can't haul him to Rock River, son."

"I know. But if you don't say nothing, maybe no one will buy him."

Dad leaned over and dropped his voice. "We need the

money, Cal. People don't have a lot of money right now and if a little salesmanship will make it easier for them to spend it, well then, I'm going to do it, for you and your mother and Jeanie. Understand?"

He didn't wait for Cal to answer, but hustled after the men.

The day after the auction, the place looked like a stripped carcass. Cal could still hear a cow or two out in the meadow, but soon their buyer would be coming to drive them away. He dragged his log roping steer out of the barn and roped it over and over, catching the horns and jerking so hard that it toppled over with every catch. The horns finally busted off. Serves it right, he thought, for being the last thing here.

"Son! Leave that and come help!" Dad was tying down the household goods in the truck bed. Cal flipped the steer over one last time and towed it to the truck. It bounced along in the dirt with its four stump legs in the air.

"What are you doing with that thing?" Jean snapped, her arms loaded with a carton of pots and pans. "We don't have room to haul that."

"Dad made it for me."

"Then what did you bust it for?"

"Jean's right," Dad said. "There's no room for it. I'll make you another one."

Cal kicked it. "There's no reason to!" he blurted. "I won't be roping anymore!"

"There'll be plenty of cattle to rope where you're going! They just won't be ours. But you wait. We'll work hard and soon we'll have enough saved to get our own again. Edie, are you ready?"

There she was looking in the mirror again, straightening the collar of her dress, pinning stray hairs in place. *They could have been halfway there in the time it took her to get ready.*

She lifted the mirror gently off the wall and Dad helped her slip it in a box. She looked behind one last time and pulled the door closed.

Mama and Jean climbed in front with Dad. Gus and Cal rode in the back, sandwiched between headboards and mattresses. Gus, ignorant that they were leaving forever, stood on a carton to catch the breeze, and Cal watched numbly as their place receded behind him. They dipped below the rim of the hill and it was gone.

He'd never been to Rock River before. What was it like? The only town he'd ever seen in Wyoming was Cheyenne where they'd gone one year for Frontier Days. There'd been crowds and lemonade stands and horses and cowboys everywhere. Even Indians. Was it like that in Rock River?

The truck chugged up the mountain pass. Cal peered through the pines, looking for elk, or maybe even mountain lions, but all he saw were rutted logging roads. Midway up the pass, one of the tires blew. Cal and Dad unloaded most of the truck just to get to the jack.

Mama stamped up and down the road, rubbing her hands together.

"It's cold, Frank."

"We're working fast as we can."

Cal blew on his own hands while his father struggled with the lug nuts. The last of the aspen leaves already littered the ground and the wind pierced his clothes. Soon after Dad pulled back on the road, Cal began to shiver.

"Get a blanket!" Dad shouted back at him.

But Cal shook his head. "I'm not cold."

"I can't think for the life of me who you're wanting to impress!"

Jean's nose was pressed against the back window. *She'd be under ten blankets and still whining if she was back here.* Gus nudged him and he sank his cold hands deep into the dog's fur.

"I hope the spare'll hold," was the last comment from Dad.

The Widow Smalls and Other Stories

A thin layer of snow blanketed the pass, and then they rolled downhill, the engine whining as they whipped around the curves. Cal scooted to the side to look over the gorges, so thrilled at their speed that he forgot about the cold. Soon the road flattened out, the trees and mountains vanished and an expanse of prairie, broad as the sky above, spread around them. The wind was stronger there, but Jean wasn't watching any more so he reached for a blanket.

The spare gave out and Dad shut off the engine.

"I'll have to walk," he said.

They all sat silently for a moment, bracing for Mama's outburst.

"You will not!" she shouted. She squared her shoulders and stared straight ahead. "Someone'll come by." They followed her gaze up the empty highway.

"You've got Cal. It'll be all right," said Dad.

"What about me?" Jean snapped.

"I want to go with you!" said Cal.

"Nobody's going anywhere!" said Mama.

Dad walked around to the passenger side of the truck, opened the door and took Mama's hand.

"We can't be too far from Harmony. If I can get help quick enough, we can be on our way and at the ranch by dusk, but if we have to sit here, no telling how long it'll be before someone comes."

"Frank, I'm asking you not to go."

"Cal, come sit up here with your mother."

"What about Gus?"

"He'll be all right back there for a little while."

Mama started to sob. "Don't leave us! Please don't leave us!" Dad gently pulled his hand away, pushed Cal in and slammed the passenger door.

Mama's sobbing would not cease. She bent over until her forehead touched her knees. "We're all alone!"

Wind gusts rocked the truck. Cal and Jean watched as Dad

grew smaller and then disappeared. Cal swallowed. With that wind yowling and Mama's sobs, his own fears prickled him.

"At least we packed sandwiches and coffee," said Jean loudly. That didn't comfort Mama one bit.

An hour later, a tow truck pulled into view. Mama dabbed at her eyes. Cal and Jean jumped out and met Dad in the middle of the road as if they hadn't seen him in a year.

He put his arms over their shoulders. "I told you we weren't far off from Harmony." He turned. "Look here — this is Burt Anderson."

The truck driver tipped his cowboy hat before squinting at their loaded truck.

"I'd say you were lucky to make it this far, buddy. Even if I get these tires fixed, they may not take you all the way with this much weight. How much farther are you going?"

"The Markham ranch outside of Rock River — ever heard of it?"

Burt shrugged. "No, but Markham, he owns the lumber mills in Laramie. Didn't know he had a ranch."

"We're going to be running it for him."

Burt sized up Mama. "You ever spent any time out here, ma'am?"

"Mister," Dad said, "you're looking at the toughest woman around!"

The tow chain clattered as Burt yanked it out of his truck. "If the wind don't pick her up and blow her all the way to Omaha."

Dad rode in the back of the tow truck for the two-mile trip to Harmony. The rest of them squeezed in with Burt.

When they piled out at his garage, Burt turned to Dad. "I know you're in a hard place, but I'll have to charge you twenty for the tow and fixing the tire and the spare."

Dad considered for a moment, reached for his wallet and peeled off the bills.

"Maybe I could work for you some while we're waiting here and you could make it ten."

Burt shook his head. "I ain't part of the New Deal. It's twenty and you can be on your way."

Dad handed him the money and nodded toward the pasture beyond the garage.

"You got a livestock tank out back, don't you?"

"What about it?"

"You're hauling water from somewhere 'cause your windmill ain't turning. I could take a look at it."

The rest of the family huddled on the east side of the garage, out of the wind, while Burt fixed their tires and Dad climbed to the top of the windmill. Cal soon grew bored watching goats peck in the town's wind-blasted yards. Mama peered through the grimy windows to check on Burt's progress and around the corner to check on Dad's.

"Your father's going to kill himself this time," she said, "Then what'll we do?"

Jean shrugged, "We could drive back home."

"Not another winter with snow high as the house," Mama murmured. "Not ever."

The tires were replaced on the truck at the same time the windmill began turning. Burt helped them reload and handed Dad back his twenty dollars.

"It's all right," Dad said. "You can keep it. We got you out on a Sunday."

Burt waved him away. "Expect you'll be coming back here overloaded again when Rock River's wore you out."

Dad started the engine and they waved as Burt returned to his garage. Then Dad got out, crossed the road and opened Burt's mailbox.

"What are you doing?" asked Cal.

"Leaving him ten. He's got to live—just like us."

Dad pulled back on the highway and Gus and Cal pressed against the cab. Although Cal had had the sandwiches and coffee, the thrill of the journey had worn off and he felt colder now. The afternoon light was puny and what little warmth it radiated was swept away by the wind.

Scattered houses marked the outskirts of Laramie, and as they slowed through downtown, Cal looked up at brick buildings blackened with train soot.

Dad turned off the main street and pulled up in front of a stone house, flanked by cottonwoods and spruces. The front lawn was wide as a hay meadow. They piled out, stiff and half-froze, and stood in the street.

Dad turned to them, "This is where Mr. Markham lives, I guess."

All of them—even Jean—ogled the gabled roof and copper gutters. Cal hadn't seen any houses like that before—not even in Walden.

They huddled on the porch under a stone archway while Dad knocked on the oak door. A tall man with auburn hair, shot through with gray streaks, opened it. He appraised them skeptically, then he opened the door a little wider.

"Mr. Markham, I'm Frank Lansing," Dad boomed.

Markham stepped aside to allow them into the entryway. For a moment, he looked overwhelmed by the bear-sized man pumping his arm. The stiffness in his shoulders signaled that he did not want them to stay.

"We've just come from church," he said, "and we'll be sitting down to lunch." He nodded toward the rest of the Lansings. "Expect you've had a long journey."

Mama took her scarf off and beamed. "We have. But to see such a lovely house at the end of the journey."

Markham bowed slightly. "Thank you, Mrs. Lansing. Maybe you can come see it some other time. You've still a ways to travel yet, another forty miles to the ranch. You'll want to be getting on."

She ignored his hint and wandered into the living room. She flitted around couches and chairs, stuffed fat as fall calves. A piano stood at the far end, next to a glass door, and she turned back to Mr. Markham.

"May I play it?"

Markham's smile tightened on his chiseled face. He cleared his throat.

"Where'd you learn to play, Mrs. Lansing?"

She'd already sat down and her fingers were rolling up and down the keys. Music filled the cavernous room. Cal's jaw dropped. Where had his mother kept these sounds all these years?

"She learned as a child," Dad explained, "in Denver."

"Denver?"

"Her papa was a cattle buyer there. I was a hand in the sale barn and that's how we met."

Markham nodded. He stood, jingling coins in his pockets, as Mama played.

"Who's playing, Daddy?"

They looked up to see a girl about Jean's age coming down the staircase. She had red hair, like her father's, rolled into sausage curls. Her eyes skipped over all of them until she got to Cal.

She looks like a doll, he thought, a dainty doll perched on a shelf, the kind that Dad used to buy for Jean before she'd broken them all.

"Laurie," said Markham, "Come meet the Lansings. They've come to work on the ranch. This is Frank and..."

"Charles Christian and Jean Marie," Dad finished.

"And that's..."

Mama beamed at Jean as she sang, "*I dream of Jeanie with the light brown hair...*"

Jean's eyes shifted away, as if ignoring her mother would make her stop.

Laurie's gaze returned to Cal. Since her eyes didn't

waver from his face, he felt like he should tell her his real name.

"They call me Cal for short."

She held out her hand. "How do you do, Cal?"

He looked down at her pale fingers. Jean elbowed him and he took Laurie's hand. He'd never touched a girl's hand before. Her grip was soft and cool.

Markham hawk-eyed them and Cal saw him nod his satisfaction when Cal released her hand.

The chords rolling from the piano began to soften. *"Never more to find her where the deep waters flow."* The last chord wavered in the air.

Mama continued to beam at Jean as she lifted her hands to her lap. "That's my baby's song."

"Mr. Markham wants us to go," Jean snapped.

"Yes," Markham said, "I'm sorry to end such lovely music, Mrs. Lansing, but if you folks don't get back on the road, you won't get there before dark."

Mama looked down at the keys. "I don't know when I'll see a piano again."

Dad glanced apologetically at Markham before tiptoeing over the rugs and touching her shoulder.

"We'll find you one, Edie. We will."

She dodged Dad's arm and reached for her coat. "Thank you so much for letting me play."

"No trouble," Markham said heartily, as he yanked open the door.

Cal looked back as he crossed the threshold. The afternoon light slanted across Laurie as she lifted her hand to wave. Before Cal could raise his hand, the door shut.

His parents were silent driving out of town. When Laramie had disappeared behind them, they turned off on a dirt road meandering through the sage. Dad slowed to a crawl, but the rocks and prairie dog holes still jarred them. He stopped where the road dove into a gully plugged with snow.

Dad pulled his cap off and rubbed his forehead.

"Are we going to go through it?" Cal asked.

"Not without a lot of digging." Dad looked up and down the gully searching for another way across. There was none. "Let's at least shovel off the top so we won't high-center."

They grabbed shovels out of the truck. Mama sat, stone-faced.

Jean said, "Daddy, I want to go on and look for the house," as she opened the door and got out.

"Get in the truck," said Dad. "Last thing I need is for you to get lost."

"I'm tired of being in the truck!"

"Jeanie, as big as you are I swear I'll wear out your bottom if you don't get in that truck!"

The door slammed loud and hard.

They shoveled snow until they were sweating.

"OK," Dad panted, "let's try it."

They jumped in the truck and he gunned the engine. They rammed the drift and for a few seconds, it seemed like they might get through, but then the tires sank and spun.

Mama got out. "We'll never get out of here before dark."

"Oh, yes we will, my darlin'. You don't have any faith in me and Cal."

"This is an awful place, Frank, just awful. Why did you bring us here?"

"It's just been a long day. It'll get better, you wait and see."

At dusk, Dad drove the truck out of the gully. They were all numb with exhaustion now. Dad flipped on the headlights. Ahead, a large corral appeared, a windmill and the house.

When he turned off the engine, no one moved. No pine trees here, no trees at all. Only wind and sage. Wind whistled around the dark house.

Dad was the first to speak. "Let's not sit here and freeze. Let's unload."

In the kitchen, Dad lit a gas light, revealing a table covered with a greasy oilcloth. Mouse droppings littered the floor.

Mama began to cry and Dad hugged her to him.

"Now, Edie…"

"Don't 'Edie' me, Frank! Get us out of here!"

"This'll be home, you'll see, Edie. We'll make it home just like where we were."

He stood rocking her in the middle of the floor while Cal hauled in wood and Jean started a fire in the stove. Cal's stomach growled, but looking at his parents, no telling when they'd let go of one another, maybe not until after he'd gone to sleep.

Gus skittered around outside, whining. Cal tried to coax him onto the porch, but he wouldn't come.

"Suit yourself," Cal said bitterly and slammed the door. He hated himself as soon as he did it. He went out again and found Gus underneath the truck. Cal lay flat down in the dirt and stretched out his arm.

"C'mon, Gus. C'mon out of there."

The dog's eyes gleamed in the dark, but he wouldn't budge. Cal gave up and went inside.

Come dawn, Gus was gone. Cal walked up the road and called and called. It was so still—not the slightest sound of life around him. He turned in every direction. His voice hardly carried. The air around him snuffed it out. The sun inched over the horizon, melting the ice in the potholes, but there was no dog to be seen.

III

Dad pulled the truck into the lean-to and the three of them — Dad, Mama and Cal — listened to the engine die. Cal's wool suit scratched against the seat with every breath he exhaled. Staring at the plank wall, he recollected Jean's train rolling into the distance, knowing that his parents' spirits were strung behind it, bouncing on the crossties like empty cans.

Without wanting to peek at her, Cal and his father waited to see how Jean's absence would weigh on Mama now, whether she would pick up and go on, or melt in front of them.

At last, she unpinned her hat from her hair and said, "I'll warm up yesterday's roast." The door creaked open, she slid off the seat and they watched her cross the yard, dust settling on her patent leather shoes.

Dad shifted toward Cal.

"It's still daylight. There's hay to put up." He trailed Mama, loosening his tie as he went.

He shuffled like an old bull, Cal thought, not like the man who, when he owned his own ranch, covered the yard from the barn to the house in three strides.

Cal waited until the porch door slammed shut. He flicked a cigarette from the pack he'd hidden in his pocket. He took a drag, set it down on the tailgate and tipped his felt cowboy hat into his palm. How proud he'd felt when Dad had first placed it on his head — it meant that day, he'd take his place as one of the men. But once Jean had retreated down the aisle, packaged for shipping in her white dress, he reckoned how shallow the pageant had been after all. Though the two of them had done nothing but fight for fifteen years, Cal dreaded the house without her.

In the gloom that had settled over the house once the couple had trumpeted their engagement, Dad had ventured, "Jeanie would have lost all interest in that boy if he hadn't a been thrown off the hay rake last summer."

Mama whipped around from the stove. "Don't give me that, Frank! I warned you if you taught her to drive she'd take detours you couldn't stop! Now you've lost her!"

Sure enough, Jean's detours to the burger joint after her university classes every day had brought about Fergus' first visit to the ranch.

It had happened in early May. Skiffs of muddy snow lingered in the yard and though the sun burned Cal's face, an icy wind kept him from shedding his jacket. He and Dad were loading the truck, getting ready to check fences. Every few moments, he glanced down the road looking for Markham. Laurie would be along to ride her horse for the first time this spring and he didn't want to miss it.

Laurie wasn't allowed to ride with Cal or his father. Dad would fetch her palomino and then she would tear around the corral, her red curls bouncing, while Markham leaned against the rail and smoked his pipe. Through the long winter, Cal had plotted on how he could take his father's place in that routine.

When at last he saw Markham's dirt plume spiraling in the distance, he jumped off the truck and shouted over his shoulder, "I'll get Buddy!" By the time Laurie's boot touched the ground, he was parading the palomino past her.

"Cal," said Markham, his head snapping back at the unexpected substitution, "where's Frank?"

"He's in the shed."

106

Markham looked confused, as if he couldn't decide whether to stick with Laurie or go find Dad.

"I suppose you can saddle Buddy for Laurie, can't you?"

Cal turned to look in those sky-blue eyes that had mesmerized him at Markham's house three years earlier.

"I guess so."

"Go with him, honey, I'll be along."

Damn. Now that he'd secured a moment with her, he couldn't put two words together!

"How are you, Cal?"

"Good."

"I haven't seen you since last fall. Did you have a good year in school?"

"On the days I got there, it was OK."

"Buddy looks so slick and shiny. Did you take care of him over the winter?"

"Yes, ma'am," he said, though he and Jean fought every day over whose turn it was to feed the horses.

Cal tied the horse in the barn and was looking for Laurie's tack when a disheveled boy, narrow-shouldered as a Brahma steer, walked into the barn.

"Excuse me, I'm looking for Jean Lansing."

From the greasy shock of hair in his eyes, Cal guessed that it had been primed and slicked back earlier in front of a mirror when no inkling of wind had ruffled the boy's thoughts. And the good shoes and slacks he wore showed he also hadn't planned on wading through ankle-deep mud.

Cal was torn. At any other time, he'd be dying to know who the boy was and why he wanted to see his sister, but at this instant, he wanted him to vanish.

"She's in the house."

"Well, I need some help." The boy pushed his hair back over his forehead. "What I mean to say is, I got my dad's car stuck in the gully back there."

The porch door slammed and there was Jean with braids

wound around her head and little pink ribbons woven through them. Cal hadn't been the only one with plans.

"Fergus!" she called out.

The boy smiled weakly and she ran across the yard.

Dad and Markham joined the barnyard huddle and Fergus retold his story.

"Don't worry," Jean said brightly, "Cal will get your car out."

No, no, NO, thought Cal. Judging by the amount of mud on Fergus, that was a job that could take hours while Laurie was here circling round and round the corral. He looked to his father for reprieve.

"Cal, go help him out."

From then on, Fergus courted once a week and skeins of fear, thick as engine exhaust on a winter morning, settled over Mama and Dad. Dad would pump Fergus' hand and ask about his parents—his father was an "Ag" professor—and his schooling—he was majoring in "Ag" at the university. Then Dad would scuttle away to the shop or corrals while Mama dished out pie and retreated to the kitchen to pull at her hair.

Cal was supposed to go with his father, but he sneaked back to the house to spy on them. He listened while they sat on the front steps. After years of enduring Jean's squawking, it floored him to hear her warble on and on like a meadowlark. He'd peek around the corner, thinking to tip Fergus off, but Fergus was bound by a spell, unmindful that he was about to lay hands on a porcupine.

Then one Sunday at the noon meal, Fergus trumpeted, "Jeanie'll be home late on Friday. After her classes are over, I'm going to take her to meet my parents."

No one appreciated his use of her nickname, except Jeanie herself, who blushed and looked down at her plate.

"What for?" asked Mama.

Fergus ignored the alarm in her tone and ploughed on. "I've been coming out here for a month now and — they'd like to meet her." He tittered and snorted slightly.

Dad bit down hard on his toothpick. "It'll be all right. This one time."

Sunup, the day after the fourth of July, Cal rode out to wrangle the draft horses for haying. He chose a pig-eared horse named Rye and they jogged for miles before he found the herd circled around a reservoir. Their heads jerked up and they quivered as he slowed Rye to a walk. He twirled his rope and whistled. Most of them towered over Rye. One kick from any of them would knock him over. To keep them from stampeding toward him, Cal threw a loop and hit the rump of the nearest fat mare. She bucked and farted and then the whole group thundered away with Rye following at a hot gallop.

Cal grabbed his hat and slapped it against Rye's flank.

"Whooo — oo — ee!" he yelled, thrilled to be rocketing over the countryside, the sage a blur beneath him.

The corral loomed ahead, severing his high spirits, and he halted with a sigh as the horses filed through the gate. Dad shut it behind them.

"Fergus has joined the hay crew," he said.

"What for?"

"Aw, Cal, he's all right." He added quickly, "Don't tell your mother I said that. I'm going to put him on the rake. Go through these horses and pick him the gentlest ones — can you do that?"

By the morning of Fergus' hayfield debut, Cal believed he'd picked the right pair. He'd chosen the two oldest ones and hitched them to the mower, figuring that dragging the mower through the thick grass would soften them up even more. Dad showed Fergus how to hitch the team up, how to drive, how to operate the rake handles and flip the fallen grass into neat rows. Then Dad joined Cal at the haystack.

Cal was perched at the top, spreading hay with a pitchfork. Down below he saw Jean, sweeping hay toward the stack, Fergus on his rake and — the buffalo.

The size of it made him drop the pitchfork. At the shoulder, it was every inch as tall as his father. It sauntered across the pasture, shaking the flies off its head, then it broke into a reluctant jog. Fergus was watching his team, watching the hay turn, just as Dad had taught him, ignorant of what was coming up directly behind him.

"Dad!" Cal screamed, but he wasn't quick enough. The team heard it — or caught a whiff of it — and bolted. Fergus leapt up and hauled back with all his might, but they were gone.

"Runaway team!" Dad shouted. It was no use. The crazed horses tore across the meadow, manes flapping, hooves pounding. They hit the irrigation ditch at full throttle and Fergus and the rake went flying.

Cal scrambled off the haystack and caught up with Dad at the ditch.

"His arm's broken," said Dad, "but at least he's alive."

Jean, who'd been kneeling by Fergus, charged Cal like a mad cow.

"You've nearly killed him!"

"I didn't do anything! It was the buffalo!"

Dad pushed his straw hat back and scratched his head. "Buffalo?" he asked.

"Another one of your stupid jokes," Jean screamed.

"A buffalo spooked them! He was right there!" Cal pointed and they turned. The only creatures in sight were teams dozing off in their harnesses.

"I hate you, Cal! I hate you forever!"

Surely his father believed him, but all Dad said was, "That's enough. Let's get him to the hospital."

No one believed Cal about the buffalo. From his hospital bed, Fergus said he'd never seen it, although he told Cal several times in front of Jean that he forgave him and knew it wasn't his fault.

Mama exploded when Cal walked back into the house.

"Get out of my house! Frank, get him out of my house!"

"The horses spooked, Edie."

"Pranks, all the time, more pranks. He never knows when to stop," she shrieked. "Get him out!"

Dad steered him outside. "Tomorrow, she'll be sorry she said that."

Dad threw two bedrolls in the pickup and they drove out across the range. A pumpkin moon peeked over the horizon, throwing long shadows behind the sagebrush. They camped by the reservoir and listened to the coyotes yipping miles away. Both of them would have shot a coyote in broad daylight, but Cal was glad they'd missed these. They were good company under this moon-washed sky. As he drifted toward sleep, he wondered what it had been like eighty years ago when buffalo, thick as stars, had roamed the countryside.

He tested his father once more. "That buffalo was big as the pickup."

"And as fast as a pronghorn," Dad muttered.

Cal raised up on his elbow, hot to defend himself again, but Dad was already snoring, his thinning hair bleached by the moonlight.

Fergus returned to the ranch in time for spring calving, and the day Cal found out Jean was getting married, they were standing over a dead calf.

"Here's what you have to do," said Cal, "you have to skin this one and put the hide on that one." He pointed to a calf snuggled in the hay, trying to sniff out what they were up to.

"Why?"

Cal took in a breath. Didn't they teach them this in his "Ag" classes?

"'Cause his mama didn't want him and the dead one's mama will take him if we tie the hide on to him."

"You want me to skin the calf?" Fergus said nervously.

"You can do it. Or I can do it."

Fergus knelt down, but his fingers trembled.

"It's OK," offered Cal. "He's dead. He's not going to feel anything. Start around the feet and peel the hide away."

Fergus slit the hide around the feet, but when he'd pulled enough loose to expose the pink flesh underneath, he retched. Cal knelt and began stripping the hide.

Fergus stopped him. "Don't. I have to do it. I've got to get used to this. I'm going to be seeing stuff like this—and worse."

"At the Ag school?"

"I've joined the army, Cal."

The army's going to take him? "What for?"

"There's going to be a war."

Cal dropped the knife as Fergus drew out a cigarette and lit it.

"Holy cow. You smoke, too?"

Fergus didn't answer. He knelt in the mud by the calf, tobacco smoke in his face. The March sun was bright and strong above and the air drifting in Cal's nostrils smelled of tobacco, of moist earth thawing and of calf hide.

"Are Indians on the warpath?"

"Why are you always joking around, Cal? Don't you

know anything? There's a war in Europe. Hitler—you heard of him? He's got Austria, Poland. He might try to take all of Europe."

"What's that got to do with us? He's not going to come here."

"How do you know?"

Cal shrugged. "Seems like one or two colors on the map would be as much as one person could handle."

"If we can't help other people fight off a tyrant, well then, who are we?"

"Have you told Jean?"

"She already knows. That's why we're getting married." Fergus flicked ash. "You're the first to know."

Cal sat back on the ground. How was he going to face his parents, knowing this news?

"What's she 'sposed to do while you're in the army?"

"She'll go with me. They've got a place for wives to stay."

Cal recalled Mama bragging about Jean at the Valentine's Day potluck supper. She'd whispered to Cal, even as the other women tired of listening to her.

"I'm the only one out here with a daughter at the university. You know that? The only one."

He glanced back up at Fergus. "Why are you telling me all this?"

"You're the easy one."

"Can I try a cig?"

"You're too young."

Cal looked down at the half-skinned calf. "You can finish that calf yourself then."

Fergus handed him the cigarette.

His mother didn't fall apart after the wedding as Cal had expected her to. She seemed at peace, even as November closed and the wind pummeled the house for days at a time. Jean's letters came once a month and she made a ceremony of opening them. She'd wash and dry her hands first, run her fingers around the envelope, then take a letter opener and slowly slit the top. She'd pinch the letter out from the envelope, unfold it and read, "Dear Mother and Dad — and Cal…" Then, to Cal's aggravation, she'd stop reading and smell the paper.

Only sixteen hundred miles' distance and Jeanie had become a saint!

The blizzards blew in, throwing up drifts against the haystacks, plugging their road to the highway — and the mailbox. With every day of snow, Mama grew quieter, as if it were burying her. She stood grim-faced at the kitchen window, vapor slowly obscuring her image in the glass.

One morning, Cal woke to daylight in his room. His father always woke him before sunup. He stumbled to the kitchen.

"Why didn't Dad wake me up?"

"I told him not to. I told him I needed you here."

"What for?"

"To get to the mailbox."

"The mailbox! We'll never get past the corrals."

Mama turned to him. "We can — and we will."

Once Cal had warmed the pickup, his mother got in. He caught the glimpse of her housedress underneath her coat.

"You can't wear that dress. You'll never stay warm."

"I'll be fine."

"We're going to get stuck. And you're not dressed to walk."

She ignored him. A hundred feet down the road he high-centered in the first drift. He glanced at her for a reprieve, but her eyes didn't budge from the mound of snow ahead of them. He shoveled furiously, rocked the truck free and within a quarter mile, he was stuck again.

After an hour, they reached the gully where Cal had

spent a muddy morning freeing Fergus' car a year and a half earlier and their own truck the year they'd come. He stopped.

"Why are you stopping?"

"Look at it, Mama! The snow's four foot deep. We'll never get through!"

"We will get through."

"I'll spend the rest of day shoveling. We'll never get to the mailbox."

"Then we'll walk from here."

"It's over a mile away! We'll freeze!"

"We'll be all right."

"Please, Mama. Please, let's go home."

Not a muscle in her face relaxed.

"Dad wouldn't want us out here!"

She turned to him. "He hauled us out here to live, didn't he?" She pushed open the door, stepped out and sunk to her hips in snow.

Cal grabbed her arm and they floundered down into the gully and up the other side. The winds slashed them and Cal thought, she'll get cold, she'll get tired, she'll give up, but his mother bent her head, gripped his hand and struggled on.

By the time they reached the highway, Cal's fingers and toes were numb. Mama wrenched the mailbox open and by its hollow ring, Cal knew it was empty.

"The postman hasn't been by!" she cried.

They couldn't see a hundred yards up or down the highway and what road they could see was streaked with drifts and ice.

"He prob'ly can't get here."

"We'll wait."

"I'm too cold, Mama."

She rocked on her feet. "I'm waiting."

Cal's teeth chattered. The cold was seeping into his bone marrow. It was useless to plead. She'd die out there before she'd give up.

In the distance, they heard chains grinding over the ice.
"That's him," said Mama.

It could be anyone, thought Cal.

"That's him."

Out of the haze, the truck emerged with the words "U.S. Mail" printed on the door. She squeezed his arm, "You see!"

The truck stopped at the mailbox and Cal forgot his misery in the embarrassment he felt as the man stared at them.

"You folks need help?"

"No," Mama replied. "We need our mail."

"What's the name?"

"Lansing."

"I don't have any mail for you folks."

She stared him down. "Check again."

Slowly, he looked down at his packets of mail and thumbed through them. "No, ma'am. Nothing here."

"There'll be a letter for me from my daughter, Jean Lansing Logan."

"No, ma'am."

Gusts rattled his truck as he and Mama peered at the mail. Cal feared she'd reach in and grab it.

After a long pause, she looked up and said, "Thanks for looking."

"Are you sure you'll be all right? You got to be miles from home." The man looked to Cal and Cal hated him for putting the two of them together.

"We're fine," Mama said. "Thanks for your trouble."

The spirit that had fired her all those miles vanished as abruptly as the postman, and Cal spent the long afternoon half-dragging her, half-carrying her back to the pickup. When they got home, he bathed her hands and feet in water warmed from the stove and then helped her to bed.

Dad came in at dusk, ice embedded in his eyebrows, and before he could ask, where's your mother, Cal dropped the coffee pot on the floor—and sobbed.

IV

Moment by moment, the wild horse race had rocketed by faster than Cal could grasp, and now, as he lay on the ground, struggling to piece it together, Laurie's face hovered inches from his own. Maybe he was dreaming, maybe he had died, he thought, and this was heaven. Yet her hair was flattened to her scalp from the cowboy hat she'd worn in the last instant he'd spotted her. So this vision had to be real.

"Are you all right?" she said.

He fished for recollections: the men and boys boosting him on the bronc, the shouts to hold on. Then they'd let go.

"Did I win?"

"Yes. But we were afraid you were going to get killed. Can you sit up?"

He studied the tiny flecks in her irises. If he whispered, she'd have to bend lower to hear.

"I'll try."

Now other men's faces crowded in over Laurie's. Was he OK? Did he break anything? Did he know that he'd won the wild horse race? Cal wished they would go away.

He sighed, "I'm all right."

Arms hoisted him to his feet, and then he was looking down at her, even though she was two years older.

"I never knew you could ride like that, Cal. It was amazing. You're always so...quiet."

"You've never said two words to me though I've hauled your horse up and down Wyoming all summer long."

The men were hustling him away and he cursed himself because he'd sounded so sulky when what he meant to say was, *just spend five more minutes with me.* He looked back. She was settling her hat, with its rhinestone tiara, back on her head. How many times had he watched her, just part of the faceless crowd, as she raced Buddy around the arena into a flying stop? It had taken this ride to get her to notice him.

She was waiting with Markham, after he'd picked up his money, the first money he'd ever won at a rodeo. Markham stepped forward and shook his hand, blocking his view of her.

"You made quite the debut here today. I didn't know you had it in you. That was a good ride."

Laurie pressed close to her father. "He wasn't just good. He was great!"

Markham paused. Her enthusiasm was excessive, more than he wanted to hear.

In deference to her, he continued, "No one thought a youngster like you would go the distance on that colt."

"Daddy, I want to ride home with Cal."

Cal thought his lungs would bust as he waited for Markham's response. Markham's tone dropped, his disapproval thrumming in every word.

"If you ride back to the ranch with him and Buddy, then he's gotta turn around and bring you all the way back to town."

"Do you mind, Cal?"

The words tripped out of Cal's mouth, even as he knew how much Markham minded. "No, I don't mind."

Once the truck doors slammed, despair knocked him square on the chin. Now that he was seeing her this close, the painted nails, the arched brows, the lace stitched down her shirt placket—all of this signaled a world much farther away from his than the forty miles between the ranch and her house.

"Why'd you want to ride with me?"

She took off her hat and the wind streaming in through the open window blew her hair around her face. She smoothed it away.

"You were right. I should have been nicer to you this whole summer. Not just because you're a great rider. You're a nice boy, Cal."

Cal dissected her statement. *Nice boy. Not a man.*

"How do you know?"

"Well, when I'm out at the ranch, I see how hard you work. Most of the boys I know in town—they don't work at all. What are your plans, Cal—after you finish school?"

He shrugged. "I may never finish. I've spent two years in ninth grade already."

"Is that because you miss so much school every winter?"

"Maybe that's the reason. Maybe I'm just dumb."

She smiled at his bait for a compliment.

"I don't know. The way you watch everything around you and take it all in—you look smart to me."

The way you watch everything—had she been watching him all the time he'd been watching her?

"School doesn't mean much to me anyway," he said. "I don't see the point in it, I guess. The ones who are paying attention—they'll get ahead—not me."

"You think you're not as smart as they are?"

"I think everyone thinks I don't need to be smart."

"What do you think?"

He glanced over at her blue eyes and her hair blowing. What could he say that would appeal to her? He'd say anything if it meant that she'd look up to him.

"You don't want to work for my daddy forever. I can't imagine you doing that."

He hesitated, then murmured, "I'd like to have my own ranch someday."

"What? I can't hear you over the wind!"

He cleared his throat. "I want my own ranch! Like we used to have!"

"How will you do that?"

"Keep working for your dad, I guess, until I can save enough."

She crossed her arms over her chest. *What had he said wrong?*

"That's a waste," she blurted. "A waste of you. You don't give yourself a chance, Cal. Your sister went to the university, didn't she?"

"Yeah, and where's she now? She's just an army wife."

"To spend years and years out here, working for Daddy — that's dumb."

How could she be so sure about what was good for him and what wasn't when all he did was tote her horse? He fretted over whether he should ask her that question or not and before he'd made up his mind, the corrals loomed ahead and there was his mama waiting in the yard.

Mama hugged herself as Laurie jumped out.

"What are you doing here, child?"

"Mrs. Lansing, you'll never guess! Cal won the wild horse race!"

Cal watched Mama while Laurie spilled the story of how a team had come looking for a jockey and how they'd begged Cal to do it and how the colt they'd wrassled had bucked and run and then bucked some more and nearly slammed into the rail, but Cal had crossed the finish line ahead of everyone.

Mama didn't hear a word.

"Honey, why are you here? He's all right, isn't he?"

Laurie glanced at Cal for help.

"I just thought — after winning the race, he shouldn't be riding home alone — that's all."

"What about your parents?"

"Daddy knows I'm here."

"Cal, you'd better get her home."

"I'll just unload Buddy." Cal gestured to the trailer.

In the barn, Laurie leaned on the grain bin while he unsaddled the horse.

"Your mother doesn't like me."

He lied. "She's just surprised to see you. That's all."

"That's not it. She didn't want me to ride with you. Just like Daddy." She paused. "I'd like to see you again, Cal. I'd like it if we could be friends."

"I'd like that, too," he murmured, but he knew that with rodeo season ending, there wouldn't be any more chances to see her.

She must have read his thoughts, for she said, "Maybe Daddy will let me ride with you on the roundup this fall."

"You think so?"

She paused. "It's our ranch, why not?"

Dust motes floated in the light slanting through the floorboards of the hayloft. She'd never ask her father. Chumming with Cal for a rodeo weekend was one thing, but not in his wildest imagination could he picture her out here. She'd thrive about as well as the daisies Mama stubbornly planted every Mother's Day only to watch them die of frostbite by the end of the week.

He reached for a brush and comb.

"I'll do it," she said. She took the lead rope from him and led the horse out of the barn.

He stood in the doorway. The sun dipped below the top rail of the corral and all he could make out was her silhouette, her arm stroking down the horse's spine. The shouts from the rodeo subsided in his mind. No cheers rocked these sagging corrals. He longed to walk up behind her, squeeze her shoulders and say, *see how these things are always here — the arc of the sun and the blue hills in the distance.*

Instead, her voice rang, "Is it always this quiet out here?"

It didn't matter that he knew she'd never ask her father's permission to ride with them. Fall roundup was more lonesome, anyway. He imagined her by his side through the foggy mornings on the mountaintops. And in the evenings, when Markham counted the cattle filing into the corral. Then her image vanished and he ached over how his dreams would never come to pass. All his days were spent with her and without her.

He caught glimpses of her when Markham hauled her out on weekends to lope Buddy around the corral. Cal would fume as Dad and Markham stood in front of the gate, blocking his way to her while deep in conversations about the fall chores. He would watch until Markham glanced at him and then he'd turn away.

In October, the snows descended from the hills to fill the corral and the weekend rides were done.

One afternoon toward Thanksgiving, when Dad had sent him on errands in town, he looked out the hardware store window and there she was, walking down the street with a girlfriend. He caught his breath and before he could decide what to do, she saw him. She stopped and spoke with her friend for a few moments, then crossed the street. The bell jangled on the door and there were her blue eyes, her grin, her red curls sticking out from under her knit cap. She untied it, pulled it off and shook her hair loose. She was happy to see him — how was he this lucky?

"Cal."

He glanced at the customers gathered at the cash

register, took her arm and pulled her down an aisle. The scuffed floorboards creaked as they squeezed between high shelves of nails and bolts.

"Why wouldn't you come see me?" she whispered, "All those times I came out—you wouldn't even wave at me."

"I thought you were coming out on round-up."

"Daddy wouldn't let me. He said if I wanted to keep riding, I'd have to stay in the corral. I thought you'd come over and say hi."

"Your dad was always there. I was afraid if he knew how bad I wanted to see you, he wouldn't bring you out anymore."

A customer squeezed behind Laurie forcing her closer to Cal so that her hair brushed his lips.

"Excuse me," the man said, and they watched him pass down the aisle before they spoke again.

"Let's get out of here," Laurie said.

The November sun sagged and the wind kicked black dust down the streets, but neither of them minded the grit or the chill. They trailed the dwindling sunlight as far as the railroad tracks and watched as the trains rocketed past. The ground vibrated beneath them and Cal felt as if they were about to be dragged away in the wake of motion and noise. Laurie looked up at him. Her cheeks had reddened from the wind and her eyes sparkled. How could he freeze this moment, how could he stop the sun and stand with her here forever?

The sun tipped at the horizon and she said, "I've got to go home."

"I'll drive you."

"No. They might see."

They walked back toward the hardware store. The buildings cast long shadows and lights glowed in the shop windows. He welcomed the dusk. Now, they were just figures to the onlookers. No one would recognize them.

They stopped next to his truck.

"I'm having a Christmas party at the house," she said, "I'll invite you."

"I'd like that."

She reached out and touched his hand. He caught her fingers and squeezed.

"I'm glad I know you, Cal," she said. Then she swiftly stretched up on her tiptoes and kissed him on the cheek, her lips ticklish as snowflakes.

The white envelope came with her address neatly printed in the corner, and suddenly he understood Mama's ritual with Jeanie's letters. He didn't want to let go of the scented paper.

He caught his mother scowling.

"It's an invitation. To Laurie's Christmas party."

"You don't need to drive to town for that. There's plenty of other girls, girls you see in the school here."

"Laurie's different."

"I said you're not going."

He leaped to his feet and looked down at her. She was just a frail, daffy old woman, after all.

"Everything you've ever asked me to do, I've done. But the only one you've ever cared about is Jean. So leave me alone!"

Mama's mouth narrowed to a hard line. "The world isn't what you want it to be, Cal, you'll see."

Her words ripped the lid off his fears and he hated her even more for that. But wasn't he holding an invitation? If Laurie wasn't allowed in his world, he could go to hers.

"She doesn't care that we work for her dad! Or she wouldn't have invited me."

Mama looked up from the invitation he held in his hand. "Go then."

At the Markhams' door, Laurie met him in a jade green velvet gown. His eyes followed the sweep of her neck down to her bare collarbone and shoulders.

"Aren't you cold?" he asked.

She smiled. "I will be if you keep standing there." She pulled him inside.

"You look — amazing."

"'A-<u>MAZ</u>-ing,'" she mocked, "Big word for a country boy who doesn't pay any attention in school. The drive wasn't too icy, was it?"

Markham watched their exchange from the doorway.

He took the pipe stem out of his mouth. "How are your parents?" he asked.

"Good. Thanks." Cal looked over Markham's shoulder. He itched to get away from him.

"And the cattle?"

Laughter from other rooms reverberated through the hall.

"Fine."

"Daddy, you don't need to be talking about that here."

Cal looked at her, relieved that she'd sensed his discomfort.

"C'mon, Cal." She took his hand and guided him into the dining room. He held back a little, overwhelmed by the scene in front of him. A chandelier glittered over an oval table mounded with food. All the girls wore gowns, like Laurie's, and the boys wore crisp suits and ties, not second-hand like his.

Laurie steered him to the group nearest the entry.

"This is Cal. His father, Mr. Lansing, works at our ranch and Cal hauled Buddy for me all summer long."

They smiled and shook his hand, with more enthusiasm than Markham had.

"I'll get you a plate, Cal, what would you like?" Laurie asked. Her chin, rounded as a china doll's — *his china doll* — was upturned toward him.

He shrugged, "Oh, anything."

She glided around the table, her long white arm reaching for slices of ham, breads, olives.

If he won this girl, where would he keep her? An image of his mother scrubbing clothes on a washboard floated between him and Laurie.

She led him into the living room, stuffy from a roaring fire. He longed to take his jacket off, but none of the other boys had. The only seat left was next to a chubby girl, Crystal, whose gown strained to contain her. Cal turned and his heart sank as he watched Laurie sweep back into the dining room. She was the hostess after all, he couldn't keep her to himself. Bitterly, he realized he'd nursed hopes for something different.

He turned to Crystal and said, "There sure is a lot here to eat."

She giggled, seeming pleased to have his attention. She glanced down and Cal realized that he was the only boy whose knobby wrists stuck out of his jacket. He tried to pull his cuffs over them when she looked away.

"This is a slow one," she said, gesturing toward the phonograph. "Do you want to dance?"

He shook his head. "No. I don't know anything about dancing."

She giggled. "You're cute, Cal." She jumped up and extended her chubby hand.

All the furniture had been pushed to the walls and the couples rotated slowly on the Persian rugs. Cal shifted from foot to foot, following Crystal. Sweat trickled down his cheekbone.

She beamed up at him, "You're doing it like an old pro. You knew how all along."

Over Crystal's head, he saw Laurie welcome another boy at the door. She kissed that boy just as she had kissed Cal a few weeks ago.

Crystal tugged on him. "Hey, cowpoke, you got to keep moving!"

126

Laurie hooked her arm into the young man's and led him into the living room.

"Luke's here, everyone," she announced

Luke was as tall as Cal. He'd doused himself with an after-shave that made Cal's nose twitch. His alligator boots shone in the firelight, and as he extended his hand toward Cal's, he removed a black felt cowboy hat.

"You must be Cal. I've heard a lot about you."

Cal dropped Crystal. He felt as if he were suffocating. By the way Laurie's arm rested in Luke's, they'd known each other a long time. What a fool he'd been.

"Those are shiny boots," said Cal.

Luke rocked back on his heels, admiring how the light played off the hide. "Thanks. They're a Christmas present."

"Looks like they've never been within ten feet of a barn."

Laurie frowned at Cal's sarcasm. "Luke doesn't have to go into a barn," she said. "He's Judge Hinson's son. And he's our class president."

Cal's voice seemed to come, not from his throat, but from off the ceiling. "How have you heard about me?"

"Well, Laurie. She says you work for her dad. It's great that you could come out tonight."

Someone put Glenn Miller on the phonograph and soon couples were whooping and swinging one another on the rugs. Wood smoke, perfume and sweat swirled through the air.

Cal watched Luke turn to Laurie. "You want to dance?" he asked and she nodded eagerly.

Cal muttered, "I've got to go outside."

"What's the matter, cowpoke?" asked Crystal.

"I'm too hot."

With Markham still in the front hall, Cal turned away and went through the kitchen and out to the back porch. A sickle moon was snagged in the bare branches of a cottonwood. He reached for his cigarettes.

The door opened and Crystal squeezed next to him.

"Brrrr! I don't know why you want to be out here."

He didn't answer. She pressed closer. Coyly, she snatched the cigarette from his fingers and took a long drag.

"I've got something you might like." She reached in her purse and pulled out a flask. "Try this."

He opened it and the warm sweet odor of burbon wafted out into the night air.

"You'd better be careful," she said, "if you've never had it before."

He tipped it back and it burned down his throat. He sputtered.

She laughed. "This is your first drink, isn't it?" She took the flask from him and swallowed some herself. "There, you see? Just a sip at a time. That's how you get it down." She wiped her mouth with the back of her hand. "See the mistletoe?" she said.

He looked up. "What mistletoe?"

"Hanging from the stars. Can't you just see it dangling above us? Whole bunches of it."

When he looked back down, her face was close to his. His lips touched hers and then she jabbed her tongue in his mouth. He was startled and nearly pulled back, but then it warmed him and he clutched her.

In the middle of the kiss, his stomach lurched. "I gotta go," he said to her.

He hustled back through the kitchen and the hall, past Markham. He jerked open the heavy front door and felt the sweat freeze on him as he ran to the pickup, knelt by the front bumper and puked.

He rose slowly and laid his forehead against the cold metal hood. The whole evening tumbled over in his head and his stomach. How had it gotten so twisted?

"Cal?" He flinched at Laurie's touch on his back. "What's the matter?"

He pulled out a handkerchief and wiped his face.

"Are you all right?"

The same words she'd used after the wild horse race.

"Yeah. I'm fine. I'm going home."

"Why?"

"Why did you invite me?"

"Because you're my friend. I wanted you to meet my friends."

"Was that it? Or did you just want to show them your hired hand?"

Laurie stepped back as if he'd struck her. "I thought you wanted to be here. I thought you wanted to see me."

Cal laid his head back down on the truck. "Then why were you dancing with him?"

"Cal! I've known Luke since we were in kindergarten!"

"Why weren't you dancing with me?"

"To start with, you didn't ask me to dance."

"You wouldn't have anyway. Not with your dad standing right there."

"You're drunk, aren't you?"

"You better get back inside. You'll get cold."

"What did you expect? That I could ignore everyone else and just be with you?"

Cal knelt at the side of the truck and heaved again. He listened to Laurie's footsteps recede up the stone walkway. Music and laughter spilled out the open door and dissipated in the dark around him. Then the door shut.

Y

Why doesn't the world look any different if all of it is at war, Cal wondered. The morning after Pearl Harbor, the sun rose and the wind kicked up snow and drove it over the range, as it had done every winter he'd been there and probably for eons before that. Day after day, the cattle plodded to the house and bawled for feed. Blizzard after blizzard blew down the sweep of the Platte River drainage, leaving behind the same drifts in the same places. Baby calves tottered around the meadows. Or froze and died — as they always had. Only when he entered a doorway and read people's ashen faces did he remember there was a war.

Jean came home in June, after Fergus was shipped overseas. Mama squawked over her at the train depot, enough to make peoples' heads turn, but Jean hardly acknowledged any of them.

"Same dirty old town," she grumbled as she pushed out of Mama's embrace.

Dad bear-hugged her, as if he could squeeze the sourness out of her.

"Of course it's the same! Don't you want it to be?"

Mama put her arm around Jean's waist, attempting to wrangle her back. "While Fergus is overseas, you can get back in school."

"Why?"

"Why, Jean Lansing Logan, because you're the sharpest, most ambitious young woman this world's ever seen!"

"That's hogwash. I don't want to hear it anymore." All three of them stared at her. "What's the point? Nobody knows what's going to happen."

"Stop that this instant!" said Mama, "You're in the same boat as everyone else! Everyone is carrying on, just as humanity's done for ages."

"None of you were there when those boys shipped out. All those boys, hundreds of them—I mean, *boys*! Going to God-knows-what. Maybe never coming home. You can't have seen that and think the world is going on the same as always. It's not going to be the same—ever. Mama, you can't tell me how to behave or what to do anymore!"

Mama planted herself in Jean's path. "You're not sitting around my house like a clump of sod! If that's your plan, go find your own ranch to rot in!"

To see them standing there, they were two sides to the same coin, both grappling to be heads up.

Jean turned to Cal so as to evade surrender. "What are you staring at!"

The next day, Mama hauled Jean to town and registered her for the fall semester, and while she waited for it to begin, Dad sent her to the hayfields. She was quieter than Cal could ever remember. After breakfast, she climbed on her rake and didn't speak to anyone for the rest of the day. She wore a straw hat with a brim so wide, Cal didn't know how she could see anything beyond the horses' butts.

It was Jeanie who made the trips to the mailbox now. She never found any letters at all, only the newspaper once a week. No one, including Mama, argued with her about who would read it first. They ceded the front porch to her where she poured over the war headlines, then left the paper flapping open on the rocker until the wind snatched it and rolled it across the yard.

At the end of a hot August afternoon, Cal watched from the barn as Jean drove up. She slipped off the seat, ripped her hat off and wiped her forehead with her shirt sleeve.

"It's hot," she pouted.

"For everyone else, too."

"What's that supposed to mean?"

"Nothin'."

"Un-hitch the horses for me, will you."

"Why can't you do it yourself?"

"I've got to help Mama with supper. You know that."

"I have a stack to level out."

Jean crossed her arms. "Mama told me about Markham's daughter. What's-her-name, Miss Laurie."

Cal shrugged.

"She said you had a crush on her and that you got invited to her Christmas party and you've been sulking around ever since. She called her a little vixen."

Cal sighed and stepped up to the nearest horse. She had counted on him unhitching horses rather than discussing this topic, and she was right.

But Jean didn't quit. "Oh-ho, you're still sweet on her!"

Cal whirled. "Why don't you leave me alone and worry about Mama? She nearly killed us, pining away for you. And all you do around here is scowl the day away. The war's not our fault, Jean!"

"Pining away for me? What do you think she'll say about these?" She whipped his pack of cigarettes out of her pants pocket and dangled them in front of him. "I found these in your jacket."

Cal lunged for her wrist. "Give me those!"

She stepped back, but not fast enough and Cal caught her wrist and squeezed.

"Ow!!"

"Let go!"

"Owww!"

"Cal, let go of her this instant!" Mama came charging across the yard. The cigarettes fell in the dust.

"What's going on here?"

Cal and Jean glared at each other. Mama bent down and picked up the pack.

"Whose are these?"

Neither of them answered.

"I said, whose are these?"

"Mine," Cal muttered.

"Vile!" Mama shrieked. "Vile, filthy habit! I won't have it. You hear me. You'll eat your supper in the barn tonight, young man!"

In all the commotion, no one heard the pickup pull in the yard until the door slammed. Cal recognized the mailman, the one they'd stopped on the road last winter. He had something this time.

The man approached hesitantly, looking each one in the eye. "Mrs. Jean Logan? I'm looking for a Mrs. Jean Logan. Is that you, Miss?"

Jean stepped forward and held out her hand. "Give it to me," she said and snatched the telegram out of his hand. She glared at Mama, as if saying, I-told-you-so, and then she ripped open the envelope.

"Missing," she said. "He's been shot down and he's missing."

Mama stepped up and took Jean's arm.

"Thank goodness, it's not the worst. There's hope."

Jean pulled away from her. "Shut up!" she screamed. "Can't you see! I don't want to live with this every day!" She leaped up the porch steps and slammed the door, leaving Cal, Mama and the stunned mailman in the sun-beaten yard. Mama stood with her lips pursed while sweat streamed down her face.

"Go get your father," she said.

Cal grabbed one of Jean's horses and vaulted on his back, relieved at the momentary escape. The horse pounded down the dirt track toward the hayfield.

The war had arrived at last.

The Widow Smalls and Other Stories

VI

On the morning of the valley rodeo, the sky was rubbed clean and only the barest breeze stirred the cottonwoods along the river. Shafts of light falling through the branches lingered on the picnic tables and food stands. The sun—along with the songbirds—was trailing south, leaving a wake of light behind. This breath of fall, with winter peeping over its shoulder, sapped the exuberance out of the festivities.

That and the War. Boys who'd volunteered were gone now and their parents sat grim and quiet among the throng. Girls swarmed around the boys, like Cal, who were left. All he had to do was lean against the Coca-Cola stand and draw them in. A year ago, he'd struggled to put two sentences together for Laurie, now he could utter nonsense non-stop and watch them giggle. Dreams of Laurie, though they still stung, were subsiding, sinking under the drift of days.

"Cal!" He heard Dad, but he ignored him for a second or two so he could keep on flirting.

"Son, come back here and sit with us." Cal followed his father's tug on his arm though he glanced back at the girls.

"Your mother's got a feast all laid out and she'd like you to eat some of it."

"I'm not hungry. I'm just thirsty."

"You've been standing there long enough to drink a vat of soda pop."

Back at the picnic table, Mama presided over bowls of potato salad, coleslaw and fried chicken. She'd put on make-up and lipstick and extended her hand to their neighbors as if she was the hostess of a mansion.

Jean crossed the grounds from the arena and slapped a number — 27 — on the table.

"What's that for?" said Dad.

"I've entered the mile race this afternoon."

Mama's head whipped around. "You've done what?" she shouted, loud enough for everyone to hear.

"I'm racing at one o'clock."

"Jean, honey — that's not appropriate."

"What are you using for a horse?" Cal chimed in.

"You're not roping until four so I can have Pee Wee."

"No, you can't! I don't want you running him into the ground before I need him!"

"All right." Dad held up his hands. "Let's slow this down."

Mama lowered her voice while glancing to see if others were listening.

"Young women with husbands missing overseas do not race horses."

"You want me to sit here with you so all these people can come up and pat my hand? Fergus may be dead, but I'm not!"

Dad turned to Cal.

"Pee Wee's got plenty of time between that race and your roping to rest up."

"You're going to let her do this?" Mama asked.

"Rest up?" Cal whined, "If she's going to ride like hell, who's to say he'll still be alive by four o'clock?"

They turned as the announcer's voice came over the loudspeakers, calling for the jockeys.

A sizable crowd had already gathered by the time Cal and his parents arrived at the starting line. Dad was tall enough to see over the crowd. Mama hung back and peered furtively between bodies. She didn't want others to notice her presence for fear they'd think she was encouraging Jean's brazen behavior.

Cal pushed to the front. Thirty riders on restless — or bewildered — horses faced the open range. Jean was in the middle. Strands of hair had worked loose from her bobby pins and wafted around her head. She held a crop in one hand, poised to whack poor Pee Wee when the whistle blew.

Cal glanced over his shoulder and jumped — there was Laurie. Her eyes were glued on him and he hurriedly turned away. The shame he'd felt the last time he'd seen her burned at the back of his neck. Since that bitter night, it had been easy to be miles away when she was at the ranch. Why had she come here now?

A revolver fired and he felt the hoofbeats of charging horses through the soles of his feet, but he didn't look up. He felt the crowd restless around him, jostling against one another, craning their necks. Had Laurie moved, he wondered? Was she still watching him? What should he do?

"Number 27, Jean Lansing Logan, is your winner, ladies and gentlemen," the loudspeaker blared.

Cal stood frozen while around him, the crowd dispersed. When he turned again, Laurie was gone.

She'd come to hand out the trophies, he learned later. At dusk, the events ended and the western horizon flared in shades of orange and blood red. Dust sifted under the arena lights. From where he sat in the bleachers, he could hardly make out Laurie's features except for the red curls falling to her collarbone. The announcer introduced her, names were called and winners climbed to the podium, but Cal wasn't listening. He was watching Laurie speak to each person, shake their hand.

Jean was so much taller than Laurie that she had to look up when she handed Jean her belt buckle. Jean held her arm out stiffly as if she wanted an arm's length distance between them, but Laurie stepped toward her, said something. Jean nodded and quickly walked away without looking back.

"She wants to talk to you," she said when she joined him in the bleachers. "She says to meet her by the chutes when she's finished. I don't know why the hell you'd go."

He didn't know why the hell he was doing it either, but his feet took him there. By that hour, night had fallen, the air had chilled. Beyond the arena, he caught strains of the band warming up on the campground. Laurie stepped out from the shadows.

"Cal," she said. She started to come closer, but when he kept his distance, she stopped. "How've you been?"

"All right, I guess."

She pulled her sweater around her and shivered slightly. "Brr, it's getting so cold. Winter's coming soon."

Light glinted off the tiara on her cowboy hat.

"Guess so."

"Every time I've come to the ranch, I've looked for you. You're never there anymore."

He looked away. "There's work to do. I can't be at the house anymore."

"I'm sorry about the Christmas party. I thought you'd want to meet my friends. I didn't understand that you'd feel uncomfortable. Please forgive me, Cal."

He shrugged and kicked at the dirt. "It's OK."

"You're saying that like you hate me."

"No. I don't hate you. We're still friends."

She stepped forward and grasped his hand. "Do you mean that?"

Cal started to pull his hand away, but she gripped it tighter until he squeezed hers in return.

"Laurie, I don't fit with you."

"I know that's what you think but you're so wrong, Cal. I like everything about you. I don't want you to be like everyone else I know. I want you to be yourself."

From the campground he could hear the band playing, *Buffalo Gals, won't you come out tonight, come out tonight...*

"What about your dad?"

She stepped closer and stared up into his eyes.

"I'm twenty years old. I can see who I want."

"I still haven't graduated from high school. I'm just a dumb nobody."

"You're wrong about that, too, Cal. You're not going to be just a ranch hand working for Daddy all your life. You are going to have your own ranch, just like you want. One day, people will look up to you just like they do with Daddy. And I want to be there for you and help you all I can. Even if Daddy doesn't like it."

He swung her arm. "Do you hear the band?"

She grinned. "Are you inviting me?"

He put his arm around her and squeezed her to him tightly as they walked into the lights at the campground. At the edge of the crowd, his parents stood watching the dancers. His father's arm hung over his mama's shoulder and they swayed to the music.

"Well, look here, it's Miss Laurie," said Dad. "You've come to the dance."

Mama leaned around Dad to glare at them.

"Yes!" said Laurie as she tugged at Cal, pulling him into the circle of light.

Now his parents' eyes turned to him and the declaration he'd intended to make to them died in his throat. He cursed himself silently. The gap between imagining himself as a man and being one widened all the time.

VII

Crusted snowdrifts crunched underneath the truck tires. The Milky Way arced above, with stars thick as pebbles in a riverbed. The truck bounced along, the headlights illuminating the dirt tracks, until Cal stopped at the edge of the bluff. Below, the town lights twinkled: whites, reds, greens. Drafts snaking in through the door frame chilled the back of his neck. He reached for Laurie's hand. She hadn't spoken for thirty minutes or more, not since he told her he'd volunteered. In the lull between them, the heater blasted lukewarm air.

The night drifted, carried by the Christmas carols, tinny and distant on the radio. When would he see this view again— this town, blazing torch-bright? After he'd gone, days would come and go and the town would remain as ignorant of the surrounding world as he was now.

Laurie stirred, her voice breaking into his thoughts.

"When will you tell your parents?"

"Tomorrow, I'll do it tomorrow."

"Daddy told you to do this, didn't he?"

"No," he answered even as he recalled Markham's words the week before: "You won't tell anyone we had this talk. Your dad, Laurie, the rest of 'em. What I've said here, it's just from one man to another. One man showing another the way."

"There's a war on," Cal continued, echoing Markham's voice in his head. "It's not right, everyone going while I'm safe here."

"I don't understand this," said Laurie.

"Don't think about it now. Just come here." Then she was in his arms, the perfume in her hair filling his nostrils.

Cal and his father had gone to the mill to pick up lumber for a calving shed that Markham wanted.

They'd stopped in his office, and as they were turning to leave, Markham had said, "Frank, leave the boy here if you don't mind." Cal and his father looked at one another. They both knew it was about Laurie. Dad shook his head before turning away — he couldn't help Cal.

A typewriter clattered outside Markham's office. Cal watched Dad outside, loading planks by himself.

"You're quaking like an aspen, boy," said Markham. "Sit down. I'm not going to chew your head off."

Cal regretted sitting where he could no longer see his father. He played with his cap, flipping the ear flaps inside and out until, under the weight of Markham's silence, he hooked it over his knee. He'd known from the first night he'd picked Laurie up at her house that this day of reckoning was bearing down on him sure as a roaring blizzard.

Markham leaned back in his chair and laced his fingers across his stomach. "I've always liked you, Cal. You know, you remind me a lot of me."

Cal wondered at those words, for all he could recall was Markham's thick veneer of disdain.

"You're clever, that's what Laurie says anyway. And I believe she's right. You work hard. And that wild horse race a couple years back — you're quite a horseman."

"Thank you, sir."

"You know I had ambition like you when I was young. And hell, look where I am now." Markham gestured expansively while his eyes skewered Cal. Those ice-blue eyes. Laurie's eyes.

"You've been dating Laurie a while now."

"Two months."

"Your parents say anything about it?"

Mama had put up a racket, though Dad had argued that Cal was entitled to follow his heart, just as they had done.

"To the ruin of himself and everyone else?" she had demanded.

"No," Cal said, "They haven't said anything."

Markham shook his head. "I can't imagine that a boy, bright as you with his whole life ahead of him, would want to stay home day after day babysitting cows when he could be out making history. This war—it's the door to opportunity for a young man like you."

The typewriter in the other room seemed to be hammering against Cal's forehead.

"Dad said I could get the agricultural deferment."

Markham snorted. "Why would you want it? Don't be a sap, son. Look at how many of the ranch boys were missing from the roundup this fall! They're out there defending our country—and securing their futures, too.

"Now," Markham continued, "we're going to win this war. And those boys coming home—they'll be heroes. Those that stayed home—no one's going to pay them any mind." Markham shoved his ashtray across the desk. "Go ahead and light up if you'd like."

Cal licked his lips. There was nothing he wanted more than a cigarette, but looking into Markham's eyes, he knew it was a sham offer.

"Take me, for instance. I'm going to be buying more land. I don't have any sons. Your dad—he's getting older. Look at him out there wrestling those planks. I'm going to be looking for a bright young man to take over my operation: the lumber mill here and the ranch. But will I look among these boys who've mewled around their mothers, or those who heeded the call? Looking at you, I see you as that young man."

Markham lit his pipe and chewed on the stem thoughtfully. "Laurie's told me your dream is to own your own ranch someday."

Cal smarted at those words. He hadn't asked Laurie not to tell anyone, but under Markham's searing gaze, the dream shriveled on the desk in front of him.

"It is," he murmured.

"It's a fine goal for a young man like you," Markham boomed.

Cal swallowed. "If I joined..."

"Ah, Cal, no one can predict the future," Markham cut in. "I'm thinking of your best interests. That's all I'm doing, son."

He and Laurie had necked on previous dates, but he was surprised by her intensity now. He pushed her away for a moment to examine her face and she unbuttoned his shirt. Then she scooted into his lap and kissed his forehead, ears, neck. She put his hand on her breast and he let it rest, hesitating to go forward. She moaned with frustration and scooted back to the passenger door.

She pulled her sweater over her head and then, with her eyes still on him, she took off her bra. White. Her skin was as luminous as the moon. And her nipples, pink and hard.

"You're shivering," he said.

"I want us to be together tonight."

Funny how his dreams were coming true, just not what he'd expected. Yes, he'd wanted this moment for years, the full owning of her at last. And he knew they were both thinking the same thing, that this might be the only moment they'd ever have.

In the back of his head, he still saw Markham's eyes, heard Markham's words. All he had to do was to get through it, to survive, and then he could come home to the ranch and Laurie. He could picture her walking down the church aisle with Markham nodding his approval.

But to have her now was to risk having her and losing her at the same time.

He looked down at the floor.

"This isn't what you want."

She cried out. "This is our last night!"

He scooted over, put his arm around her and pulled her to him.

"I don't want you to have it this way. Me on top of you on this greasy old truck seat. I want to think of you back here, looking at my picture every day. I want to think of how it'll be when it's over and I come home."

She pulled away from him, reached for her sweater and tugged it back over her head.

"You don't want a woman, Cal. You want a doll to sit on a shelf while you go to war. Do you think that I can stop the world from turning while you're gone?"

Cal looked out again at the lights. "I'm doing this for us. So we'll have a future. If I stay here, we won't have one."

"You've signed our future away! Now there's only right here, right now."

"I won't believe that," he said. Then, "Will you come to the station? Will you see me off? Please."

She came back over to him. He stuck his hands underneath her sweater and ran them up and down her back.

"Just come to the station. Please be there."

He wanted her so much he could explode.

VIII

Cal fumed as he scanned the line of families at the train depot. Where was Laurie? A Christmas tree, smothered in tinsel, claimed the far corner, but there was no merriment in the hushed voices that reverberated through the waiting room. Under the dull globe lights, all the boys looked pale and all the parents, lined and hollow-eyed.

Mama and Jean stood next to him in their coats and mufflers, stone silent. His father wasn't there.

He hadn't told Cal he wasn't coming until the day before. They'd fed the cattle together, as they'd done every morning of every winter. The wind was blowing hard, driving frozen grit into their faces.

"I'll drive," said Dad. "You feed."

"It's my turn," said Cal, knowing his father would get chilled sitting on the seat in the wind.

Dad waved him away. Cal pitched hay and every few moments glanced at his father's hunched back. Markham's words rattled round his head—your dad's getting older. For the first time in Cal's life, he would be out here alone from now on.

Dad halted the horses when the wagon was empty.

Behind them, the cows munched their hay in long rows, the wind flattening their long winter hair. Dad sat motionless and Cal feared that something was wrong. He jumped off the wagon and walked to the front.

Dad pulled out his handkerchief and blew his nose.

"I can't go with you tomorrow. I'm sorry. I can't do it."

"Why not?"

His father sank his head into his huge hands and sobs rattled him so hard that the seat shook.

"You're my only son!" he sobbed.

"You're talking like I've died. I'm standing right here."

Dad wiped his eyes. "We've had no news of Fergus. We don't know if he's dead or alive. Now you're going off, too."

"That's not going to happen to me."

"How do you know that?"

"Fergus didn't have Jean around all his life to toughen him up like I did."

Dad laughed and wiped his tears away. He pulled Cal to him. Cal tried to pull away, but Dad wouldn't let go. The cattle cleaned up the last shreds of hay and broke for water. The sun climbed higher above them, the moments ticked by. His father hugged him ever tighter.

Mama and Jean were closer to the sign-in table now and still no sign of Laurie.

"I'm going outside to look out for her," Cal said.

Just then the door opened and Markham appeared in a whorl of snow. At last, thought Cal, but Markham was alone. Snow dusted the collar of his overcoat. He turned to shake hands with families at the end of the line. Cal listened, straining for some word of Laurie. He could hear the tones of voices — the exchange of holiday greetings and Markham's wishes of good luck — but he couldn't make out their words.

Cal's heart raced as Markham worked slowly up the

line. He fought the urge to run to him and demand where Laurie was.

When Markham reached them at last, he ignored Cal and grasped his mother's hand instead.

"Edie, how good to see you. I know this is a hard day for you."

Mama's eyes filled, but before she could respond, Jean spoke up. "Where's Laurie?"

"Cal," said Markham. He took Cal's hand and shook it warmly.

"Where's Laurie?" Jean asked again.

Markham turned like a man harried by a yapping dog.

"I'm afraid she couldn't make it. She's getting ready to leave for Chicago in a few days."

"Where?" Cal whispered hoarsely.

Once she'd whispered the promise in his ear, that she would be here, he'd believed their future was steady and sure as a beacon on a winter's night.

"She got a job working for a newspaper. They may turn her into a reporter. She'll start out emptying wastebaskets, I guess, until she works her way up." Markham shook his head. "Helluva world now for women, don't you think, Edie?"

The light in Cal's mind went out. Now when he returned —*if* he returned—he'd be the ranch hand again. That's all he'd ever be.

Jean snapped. "You've crammed a load of manure into Cal, that's what I think."

"Jean!" Mama gasped.

Others in the line turned to stare at them, but Jean ignored them.

"What did you come here for anyway?" she blurted.

Markham's smile was as taut as newly stretched barbed wire. "To see Cal get on that train. As I know he will."

They were at the sign-in table.

Jean turned to Cal. "You don't have to go," she said.

"Name?" said the gray-haired woman at the table.

Cal looked down at the hand-written names on the long roster.

"Charles Christian Lansing."

Each of the draft board members at the table shook his hand.

"Best of luck, son."

"Knock 'em dead."

"Come home soon."

"God bless," said the gray-haired woman to his mother.

Mama grasped the woman's hand. "You don't know how very proud I am of this boy," she whispered.

Cal whipped around to stare at her. Strange to hear those words for the first time.

Then he noticed that Markham had gone. He looked down the line and couldn't see him anywhere.

The murmurs rose and Cal stared out the window. The train had arrived. Families filed out to the platform and a cold draft swirled into the room.

Jean gripped his arm. "Listen, Cal. Do you hear me? You don't have to go!"

Blowing snow was forcing the parents to curtail their farewells. They surrendered their sons to the waiting train and pulled their mufflers tight around their mouths as they helped one another away.

Faces filled the train windows, some dazed, others excited about the journey and the prospect of adventure. So many faces, more than Cal could count.

Cal took his mother's hands and held them. "I'm ready to go."

"Cal!" cried Jean.

Tears spilled out of Mama's eyes. "Let him choose, Jean."

"I'll write."

Mama wiped away the tears with the back of her hand. "I'll check the mailbox every day."

Cal turned to Jean. "You'll need some warm gear for those mailbox trips."

Jean threw her arms around Cal's neck. "Bring Fergus back with you."

They trailed after him to the platform, the wind tugging at their headscarves.

"Don't wait out here, go inside," he shouted back at them, but they stayed, arms locked together as he boarded. When he, too, pushed his face against the window, they were still waiting.

Slowly the train pulled away. Jean let go of Mama and ran alongside. She tried to keep waving, but the wind was too strong. She kept running with her head lowered. She ran until the platform ended and the car swept past her. She jumped up and down, waving.

He watched until he couldn't see her anymore, until everything he'd ever known was no more than snowflakes swirling over the iron tracks behind him.

Jamie Lisa Forbes

The Widow Smalls

Jamie Lisa Forbes

The Widow Smalls and Other Stories

I

The thud of gravel battering the coffin made her jump. Leah glanced back at the Hanson boy to see if he'd noticed. She was embarrassed by her reaction, the squeamishness of it. After all, she'd been watching the backhoe ever since the mourners had dribbled away. The boy had warned her. He'd suggested she might want to follow the others, but she'd brushed him off. She would be just fine, thank you.

The boy shifted from one foot to the other, pretending that he hadn't noticed. Unblemished by life, or death, he aspired to decorum as he stood with his hands crossed in front of him. Like all the boys in this town, his neck and face were sunburned above the collar. She was certain he was suppressing a smirk.

The backhoe reached for another load. It wasn't the sound that had startled her, but the reality coming to roost, the weight of the earth showering down on her husband of thirty years. If she'd gone first, Bud wouldn't have fretted. He had buried innumerable animals this way. Yet for her, the sound was a shove into a blurry future.

The boy coughed loudly. Maybe he did have something in his throat, but Leah heard it as another prod to shoo her back down the path to where her brothers-in-law waited. He wanted to pack this canopy up and get on to his father's next job. Old man Hanson understood that a combined excavation and funeral business would pinch sensitivities, even among the practical in Thistle, Wyoming, so the businesses were listed separately in the phone book. But the Hansons always looked harried at funerals. The rituals of death siphoned off precious equipment time.

Leah took her handkerchief out of her purse. She wasn't crying, she hadn't cried from the moment she'd seen Bud lying inert. Widows clutched handkerchiefs, didn't they? Didn't they lean on their childrens' arms as they were led away?

Leah had no children. But she needed something to clutch in order to shift her from this spot where her knees were stiffening and her feet swelling. She brought the handkerchief to her face and inhaled her perfume, *Gabriella*. She could picture Gabriella on her TV screen, flouncing her volumes of hair on a beach far away from Thistle. Inhaling the scent was a comfort, a comfort to know that Gabriella was out there, untouched.

She turned to the Hanson boy and said, "Sorry. Sorry I've taken so much of your time."

He looked relieved. "Don't you worry, Ms. Smalls. You take care of yourself."

She stepped out from under the canopy into sunlight so intense that she winced. There'd been no spring this year, unless you could call a couple of rain-filled potholes spring.

They had rocketed straight from the last blizzard into dry heat so unrelenting it had already withered her petunias. Once they'd flopped over in defeat, she had stopped watering them, but she'd left them in their pots. Revive or not, they were damn well going to stay there until Labor Day.

Now, with Bud's passing, she had a good excuse for not removing them. If curious neighbors trekked out on the pretense of paying their respects, they wouldn't depart clucking about her neglect. "Poor Leah" — that's what'd they say — "so overcome she can't pull up her dead petunias."

Leah looked down the path to the dirt parking lot below. Now her eyes did tear at the light bouncing off the roof of Merle's emerald Lincoln. Merle fanned himself with his cowboy hat. Grady stood, feet apart, with his hands in his pockets. She knew they were fuming. Her dilly-dallying was keeping them from their loop of ranch chores, chores that the Smalls brothers, Bud included, had never tired of prattling about. They could entertain themselves for hours over how to clean a ditch.

More importantly, she was keeping them from the platters of food their wives had prepared back at Merle's house. The rest of the funeral party would be lingering there over the deviled eggs, waiting to fulfill their obligation to squeeze her hand and murmur phrases fresh from the insides of sympathy cards. As she squeezed her eyes shut, she could picture the entire group as a line-up of life-size condolence cards.

She tried to smile and wave to Merle and Grady — the "boys" as their mother had called them even at the tail-end of her dotage. They didn't wave back. Her heels skidded on the gravel as she inched down the path. She understood why the town fathers had planted the community graveyard up over the hill. That way the passersby — cursing as they braked from eighty miles an hour to thirty — would see signs of life in Thistle instead of death. But it was another matter as to why generations of mourners were forced to scramble up and down a goat path. There's a message: death, as well as life, had to be a challenge in Thistle.

Neither Grady nor Merle stirred to help her. She could pitch head long down this path and wind up at their feet with her pantyhose ripped and they wouldn't budge.

Just then Grady called out, "D'ya need some help?"

"I'm all right." She turned her hip to them and side-stepped down the hill.

Beyond the parking lot, Thistle's buildings hunkered along its main street. She watched its traffic light switch over and over again through the turtle-crawl of her descent. Beyond the town ran the railroad tracks guaranteed to make memories of Thistle no more than a sneeze.

Now she needed her handkerchief because of the sweat trickling down her face. The scent had evaporated.

She called back down to the boys apologetically. "If it'd been me, Bud never would have made it down this hill in his cowboy boots."

Grady answered while Merle fanned himself. "You're right. He'd a croaked right there, instead of in the bedroom. You're gonna make it."

In the last few feet, Grady held out his hand as she stepped down to him. She grasped it and squeezed—just a reflex—but he squeezed back. Then he dropped her hand abruptly so he could reach for the soda can on the car hood and spit his tobacco wad.

"Let's go," said Merle, "it's as hot as hell out here."

The "boys" got in the front and left Leah alone in the back. The hot leather seat seared the back of Leah's thighs and she tugged at her skirt, trying to stretch it down. She felt choked by the abrupt strangeness of everything.

Bud was not beside her anymore to do all the talking. Merle, who had always listened to Bud with a tortured expression, as if Bud were standing on his toe, was now the eldest. He was going to be the leader of the family. Where was she going to be? Taking a back seat.

She dabbed at her face again.

"You're right, Merle. It's really hot."

Merle glanced at her in the rearview mirror before swinging out onto the highway.

It was dusk before she inched her own car up the rutted lane she'd always hated. The gathering at Merle's house had boosted her, swooshed her aloft, but as funeral guests departed, her spirits gushed out of her like a fart, until she'd bolted out of fear that anyone who remained would hear it.

People she hadn't seen in ages came, even the Joliettes, who'd moved to Sheridan. She'd gone to high school with Pam who'd been such a slim young thing. What a surprise to see that she'd plumped out like Leah, herself. They'd embraced and rocked together until everyone stared and then they'd sat down, forgetting the paper plates on their laps, and talked about old times: how they used to make fun of the ranch boys in school, how funny it was that they'd become ranch brides themselves, and all the adventures they'd had settling into ranch families who'd considered them too spoiled and frivolous to be of any use. Oh, but they'd stuck it out. Yes, they had.

And Pam had brought pictures of grandchildren. Grandchildren for gosh sakes! Thirty years on the ranch with Bud and whole generations had come up. Leah had thought she'd been aware of the seasons passing, but eventually they'd all compressed together into one long scroll where nothing in particular had occurred.

She parked the car by the porch door. Bud had always

squawked when she did that. "Leah, what's that car doing out?" He'd wanted the car in the shed thirty yards away even if she had groceries to unload, and then she'd have to hike back and forth, hauling paper grocery sacks that invariably split open.

She wouldn't ever hear that again. From now on, this car was going to be nosed smack against the porch until they hauled her carcass out of there.

Bud's dog, Pepper, came up to her, flopping her tail and snuffling her shoes and dress. He'd brought the dog home in the huge ham of his arm when she was a pup. She'd perked her tiny ears as Bud cooed at her.

Now Pepper sniffed around the car, looking for him. How long would she look? How many days would pass before Bud's odors would fade?

Leah went inside and flipped on the kitchen light. *Until they hauled her carcass out of there...* What would become of her? She had nowhere to go. Many Thistle folks left their places to their kids, or sold them and moved to Arizona. Every year those Christmas cards came. By then, the Smalls would have had two or three months of winter, but in the Arizona photos, aqua pools glimmered among pots of bougainvillea. She and Bud had clucked over how fantastical it seemed.

She could do that. She tried to imagine herself in a realtor's car, gliding past each yard with a "For Sale" sign, studying each little walkway leading toward doors of possibility.

The image dissipated. This kitchen had always been her refuge. This kitchen, with its hand grime on the drawers, the rooster clock, the cabinets still coated with the same butter-colored paint she'd slapped on them when she was twenty-five, the dripping faucet that Bud had sworn he'd fix—but somehow it had never gotten fixed, not ever in thirty years—and now it never would. She turned off the light and focused on the sounds familiar to her: the clicking of the minute hand on the clock, the hum of the refrigerator. An owl hooted from the windmill outside.

Until they hauled her carcass out of there.

Dawn found her still at the table. She rose, started coffee. She put on her tattered sweater and stepped outside into the morning chill. It caught her by surprise and she shivered. Moisture beaded on the car hood—let Bud turn over in his grave! She ambled half way across the yard, then stopped.

It was light enough to view the ranch—now *her* ranch: barn, bunkhouse, calving sheds, machine shed, corrals and in the rising light, the plains beyond.

In the hustle and bustle of death—the flurry of phone calls, the business and funeral home trips, the visits from the Smalls' wives bearing casseroles she would never eat—she had entirely forgotten the ranch. Cows lowed for their calves. Cows. She owned over two hundred of them. Had Bud awoken this morning, he'd have already been out checking water tanks and pastures. Come Fourth of July, he would move the hay machinery out from the machine shed. Haying—hay to put up. Who would do it?

Slowly she turned to take it all in. It was true what Bud used to say—*a ranch doesn't stop for nothing.* That had always been his answer when she'd ask if they could get away.

"Anything. You mean a ranch doesn't stop for anything," she'd snap. "And that's just an excuse. It's got nothing to do with the ranch. You can't stand to leave your brothers for two minutes!"

By God, he'd been right. A ranch does not stop for...

Leah bent over and retched.

An hour passed before a dust skein rolled up over the sagebrush. Visitors. A reprieve from the fear threatening to crush her. She checked her face in the mirror, touched her hair. She had to pull herself together. Dead petunias were one thing. Her physical appearance had to conform to sensibilities. No one felt sorry for you if you didn't look your best.

It was Merle and Grady. Thank God. They must have been thinking of it, too — how Bud's ranch would carry on. They had come to help her figure it out. Better yet, they'd take over. They'd want some fee for managing the place, a percentage of the calf sales, maybe, but that would be all right, just so long as she could stay here and take her time.

Pepper was already snuffling Grady's boots, still looking for Bud. Grady grimaced and tried to nudge her out of the way with his foot.

Merle rapped on the screen door. He took off his sunglasses and peered inside.

"Leah, you there? Can we come in?"

"Yes, the coffee's hot." She was so happy to see them that her heart fluttered. How silly she'd been. They were family. They wouldn't allow her to go belly up here by herself. Why had she been so upset?

Odd that Merle skulked like a dog with its tail between its legs as he came in. Grady wouldn't look her in the eye either. His gaze flew all around as if he was studying the house, measuring it. Why? He'd been here a thousand times.

They plopped down and said nothing while she hustled with their coffee. Once she'd laid out sugar, milk and graham crackers, she sat down across from them, hopeful, expectant to hear how they planned to rescue her.

Merle crossed his arms over his chest. Grady was entirely occupied stirring his coffee. The spoon clinked over and over.

"We know you've been through an awful shock," said Merle, "but do you know you got fence down all along the road? Your cows are out of grass—they should've been moved to the Ely Creek pasture two weeks ago. Have you thought about what you're going to do?"

Leah stared at him, knocked off kilter by the detachment in his tone. Had she ever talked to these boys without Bud? Her mind zipped back to her wedding where the boys had tittered and horsed around at the altar. As everyone's attention had shifted toward them, the haze of love had lifted momentarily and she'd balked at "I do." At the time, she thought the steadiness in Bud's eyes had swept her on. But really she'd been carried along by the current of expectation in the crowd behind her.

After that, it was always Bud, Merle and Grady in a huddle. She was relegated to the kitchens with the rest of the wives, not to be resummoned until their stomachs, or other appetites, demanded. In all this time, she'd never spent five minutes alone with these boys.

"I...thought you two would run it. It would be so easy. Your places are right next to mine." Her voice sounded raspy.

Grady cracked a graham cracker in half. The crumbs sprayed over the table. Merle glared at him, annoyed, and waited for the chewing sounds to subside before he went on.

"We're not interested in running a place we don't own. Last we heard, you got this place."

Leah clasped her hands in her lap.

"Well, Bud never did do a will. The way I understand it, the way it's been explained to me, yes, it's all mine. I just... well, this house has taken up all my time." She waved her hand vaguely around the kitchen until, under their gazes, it dropped. She forced a little laugh.

"I just never planned on running a ranch. I thought we'd retire."

Merle nodded. "You're right. Bud shoulda thought this whole thing out better, what with no kids to take over. He shouldn't have left you high and dry. But that's not our fault."

"You've got boys of your own. Surely they can help out. I'd pay them. I'd give them a percentage, whatever you want." Grady wiped his fingers on a napkin.

"That's not what we have in mind. What we were kinda hoping is that you'd want to sell. I mean…it's like you said, our places surround yours. Whatchya want to stay here for? There isn't anything a'tall to hold you. You could go on to some place nice, like…Arizona."

"We've come over here to help you." Merle chimed in, "We think the best solution for all concerned is that you sell the place to us."

They aren't asking — it's already decided. Somewhere, there'd been another huddle and now their faces were as hard as rock.

"Oh." Leah straightened in her chair. They all sat there like lumps while the bluebottle flies, trapped on the window sill, buzzed and hurled themselves against the screen.

Grady stretched and crossed his legs. The flies were annoying him. Had the conversation not run aground, he'd be asking, "Leah, got a market for those flies yet?" And there would have been the usual guffaws from Merle…and Bud.

"What do you say, Leah?"

"I don't know. I mean, what are you boys willing to pay?"

Grady and Merle looked at each other again — code talk, she realized. Merle reached in his shirt pocket, pulled out his notepad and slapped it on the table. There was already a figure written in pencil.

"What's this for? The land?"

"No," said Grady. "Everything — cattle, land, buildings, machinery, everything."

"The Craddock place near town sold for more than this last year."

Merle sighed heavily.

"The Craddock place was bought by a mining company for the gravel. This place isn't going to bring that kind of price. I know you're not in your right mind due to grievin' and all, but you got to wake up. You'd be waiting for years and years to get that kind of price. If you ever get it."

"Don't speak to me like I'm feeble-minded. You think I haven't been listening to the market reports for thirty years? You don't think I know what those cows are worth?"

"Who's going to gather them for you?" asked Grady. "Have you figured in your trucking cost?"

Bzzzzzzz. The sound was hollowing out her brain. She glanced down at the figure again. "I don't have to take that."

"No," said Grady, "you don't."

"I can put the place up for sale myself. I can get a better offer. You think I don't know you boys, but I do. You need this place. You'd hate it if some strange outfit moved in. You're always going on about how your daddy wanted all these ranches to be run as one."

If they looked at one another one more time, she'd slap their heads off.

Grady turned back to her.

"You're right, Leah. You can sell this place yourself."

These boys needed to leave, shuffle to the door, toot back down the road. She was ready to watch the dust cloud obscure any trace of them.

"Who's going to put up your hay while you wait for a buyer?" asked Grady.

"Come to think of it," said Merle, "the water on the meadows needs to be shut off. That is, if you want to start haying in a few weeks."

"If Bud heard the two of you now, he would roll over in his grave. He was always helping you out. Always."

"Fact is," said Merle, "if it had been us, he'd have said exactly the same thing to our families. He had a good head for this business. He always understood what needed to be done."

"Let's leave it alone for a while," said Grady. "I got my own haying machinery to work on." He stood up.

Merle leaned forward and rested his hand on her knee. "This is a lot for you right now. You think on it. Take as much time as you need. When you're ready, give us a call."

"It's your ranch," Grady said, as he pushed Pepper out of the doorway. "You run it best as you see fit."

11

A falcon whistled overhead. Leah swung around anxiously, trying to spot where it was headed. She didn't want the damn thief raiding her chicken house. There— he'd settled on a fence post.

"Shoo, shoo, get out of here," she shouted. The bird blinked. "Go get him, Pepper." Pepper looked up and wagged her tail. Leah hustled toward the bird and it spread its wings, swooping low to the ground before catching the updraft, and then it was up over the corrals and gone.

There was no time to stand around gawking anymore. She had a ranch to run.

She ticked off the events Grady and Merle had mentioned: move the cattle, shut off the irrigation headgates. The haying machinery…she could ask at the service station. Maybe someone would be willing to come out in the evenings and get it ready. And in two weeks, maybe she could find some help for haying. Surely there were ranch boys out there somewhere looking for summer jobs.

First, the cattle. She looked over the horses in their pasture next to the corrals. This was as close as she had been to them in years. She used to drive cattle with Bud, but that had ended abruptly one June, early in their marriage. He'd snapped at her for the third or fourth time about pushing her end of the herd.

"God gave you heels, girl. Can't you boot that fat horse and push those calves up?"

"I'm doing the best that I can! They won't move!"

"You're not doing anything to move them. You're no more than a sack of potatoes in that saddle."

"I don't need to be out here. If you don't like my help, move these cows yourself!"

And then a torrent of wind and hail smacked her so hard it took her breath away. She dropped her reins and put her arms over her head.

"Leah, get the slicker off the back of your saddle!" Bud shouted.

She dismounted. The hail pummeled her as she tried to shelter against the horse's flank. She could still hear Bud shouting, but she couldn't make out what he was saying. She reached up to the back of the saddle and tried to untie the saddle strings.

"Bud, help!" she sputtered.

Both he and the cattle were gone. All she could see and hear was the driving hail.

"Bud!" she screamed.

She struggled into the slicker and climbed back into her wet saddle. The seat of her jeans quickly soaked through. Hail pellets ran down her shirt collar. Her teeth chattered. She'd never been so cold, not even on winter days when she'd gone out to feed cattle with him. At least then she'd known it would only be an hour or two before she could warm up back at the house. There was no end to this, no shelter in sight.

I'm going to die out here.

She let the reins run slack and the horse ambled on. She tried to glance up every few moments, and, at last, she made out Bud in front of her, still trying to push the lead cows into the storm.

His indifference to her magnified her torment. She sobbed.

"I'm soaked. And freezing. I could have gotten lost. Don't you care about me at all?"

"While you sit there and blubber, the cattle are scattering all to hell!"

Thirty days later they still weren't speaking. They'd gone into town for Merle's birthday party at the Roundup, and once everyone had knocked back a few drinks, Merle had punched *A Good-Hearted Woman* into the jukebox. The brothers and their wives hustled to the dance floor, leaving Bud and Leah alone. Leah rested her chin in her hand and looked out at the dancers. Bud rolled a toothpick between his thumb and forefinger and then picked his teeth. He shifted and eyed her head on. His eyes sparkled with that sly twinkle, the look that had first drawn her to him. His forearm dropped on the table, palm upwards, a gesture of surrender.

"How 'bout it, toots?"

With the Tequila Sunrises she'd had, and the music, and the brothers sashaying over the dance floor, the fight didn't seem worth the effort anymore. She'd dropped her hand in his and he towed her out among the dancers. As she pressed against him, she inhaled odors that she'd missed: wind and dried sweat.

But she had never ridden again.

Now, she decided the swayback buckskin, Amos, was her best bet, only because he was the oldest and least likely to give her any trouble. Then, a saddle. Among saddles coated with dust, Bud's was the only clean one. She jerked it off the rack, not realizing how heavy it was, and it yanked her to the plank floor. She dragged it by the horn over to Amos.

Without the slightest effort, Bud would have swung the saddle up and over the horse's back. The image was so vivid to her she could hardly believe he wasn't there. She could feel him shouldering her out of the way. "Give me that thing, Leah." But when she looked over her shoulder, no one was there and beyond the open door, the only presence was the wind sifting eddies of dust in the yard.

In the end, she had to fetch a stepladder, haul the saddle up and drop it on Amos' back. As she fumbled with the cinch, trying to remember just how the damn thing hooked up, Amos looked back at her with liquid brown eyes.

"No point in you looking for him—he's not coming back." The horse turned away and sighed deeply. The end of Bud could no more be imagined than the end of wind and grass and sun—as far as Amos was concerned, anyway.

Once she'd mounted and rode out into the sunlight, she felt buoyed at her achievement. The sun was a twinge hotter than it had been thirty minutes ago, but Merle and Grady be damned—she was ready to move cattle on her own ranch. Pepper trotted alongside her and wagged her tail, as if catching Leah's mood. *Whoopee-ti-yi-yo!*

They plodded across the range. The swelling heat had cleared the air of songbirds and sucked up the last traces of dew. Prairie dogs poked their heads up out of their burrows and eyed her.

As the sun pulsed, the pasture expanded before her, rolling on and on to the vacant horizon. Had Bud ever felt dwarfed by this space? His ego had never allowed room for that thought. He'd filled every room he entered and made sure everyone knew it. And his inner meditations had never been among his conversation topics. If he'd ever felt defeated, he'd never shared it with her. Funny how she couldn't get him out of her head when she'd been so locked out of his life.

At last, up and over the butte, the fence line appeared.

Twenty or so cows and calves lay at the gate, flies swarming over their backs. Some rose and stretched as she and Amos approached, all of them looked at her expectantly. From habit, they knew if they sat and waited long enough, someone would come along and open the gate. Maybe when the rest of the herd noticed, they'd come, too.

"Just a minute, mamas," she said. "Just give me a sec."

She pressed her shoulder against the gate post, reached up and tried to push off the overhead loop. Damn, it wouldn't budge. And how had a lifelong rancher's wife forgotten to bring gloves? She yelped as the barbs jabbed her hand.

Yet another of Bud's legacies: gates that only God's thunderbolts could open. And then he'd had the nerve to gripe when she hadn't closed them. She cursed him while she shook the pain out of her hand. The cows looked on, their ears flicking back and forth.

Leah thought to look in his saddlebags—sure enough, a pair of wire cutters. I'll show you, Bud, you damned bastard. She snipped the top loop and the gate crashed to the ground. She looked back at her cows and threw her arms up in victory, as if they'd applaud. Instead, they rose, plodded through the opening and sank their heads down in the new grass.

Only two hundred and some to go. Plus the bulls.

Leah goaded Amos into a jog and they zig-zagged back and forth across the pasture, charging into little knots of cattle. The groups ambled a few feet to appease her and then shrugged her off, as if she was just another pest to contend with. By mid-afternoon, the heat had wrung her out, and Amos stumbled from exhaustion. And she hadn't thought to bring water. For all their effort, they'd succeeded in pushing only a dozen cattle or so through the gate.

She thought back to how the day had begun with Merle and Grady. So far, she'd spent the entire day proving their point. Just as they'd said, she couldn't manage. She felt naked under this sun, exposed for the fraud she was. She longed to be in her kitchen with a glass of iced tea, even though the kitchen itself would be stifling hot at this time in the afternoon.

Amos broke into a jarring lope toward home, his mane flapping with each stride. She dropped the reins and gripped the saddlehorn. Let those boys mutter against her. If she could just have that glass of iced tea, she'd never want anything else. She'd rattle the ice until she'd knocked the Smalls brothers' voices from her head, until the only sound would be the rooster clock ticking away the hours.

And then it would be tomorrow.

A couple days of sunlight ebbed and flowed from her kitchen window before some gumption ignited in her. Sipping her iced tea, it occurred to her that she had to emulate Bud: get up when the stars were still thick outside and start work before the sun could sap her energy. Using that tactic, she gradually moved all the cattle, except for a cabal of bulls who drooled and snorted every time Amos approached.

One week later, at daybreak, she was back at the gate, puzzling over how to fix it.

However it got fixed, it would be a new day at the Smalls ranch, she decided. Gates would open and close with ease. Bud's toolbox lay open at her feet complete with wire stretchers, a roll of wire, hammers and staples. She had everything she needed to tackle her job. She'd even remembered gloves.

First she fashioned a new loop for the gate post, making it longer than the old one so it would be easier to drop over the gate. She nearly busted with pride as she pulled on her leather gloves and hammered the new staple into the post. Her ranch, her gloves and soon, a gate she'd actually fixed and closed.

But Bud's gate was so tight she couldn't stretch it across the opening. She tugged on it until her shoulders ached. She let it sag, took a big breath and jerked it hard as she could, but still it wouldn't reach the post. Her new loop just dangled there, waiting. She cried out in frustration and let the gate collapse in a tangle of wire.

An engine was buzzing somewhere. Oh God, Grady and Merle. She looked up and saw a motorcycle in the distance. Couldn't be them. They'd be in their pickups. She tried to make out the figure as he approached. Trespasser, maybe an illegal hunter out to bag an antelope. By now, it was probably slapped on some highway billboard that she was here alone. And her only weapons of defense were the tools at her feet. She picked up the hammer.

The man stopped. Underneath his cap, his skin was dark. Not just sun-tanned. Mexican, that's what he was.

"I'm Leah Smalls. This is the Bud Smalls Ranch, and I'd like to know what you're doing here."

The man took his cap off and nodded politely. He was older than she'd supposed at first glance. His shoulders were broad and his hair was close-cropped and gray over his ears, though thick and black on his crown. The squint lines around his eyes told her he worked outdoors. A working man's face, all right. Yet his eyes were warm and expressive, not clouded with any of the middle-age tedium she was familiar with.

"I stopped at Merle Smalls'. He said you might need some help for haying." He glanced at the tangled gate on the ground. "Maybe you need some other help as well?"

Merle would be cackling at this instant. He knew Bud would never have stood for a Mexican hired hand.

"I don't believe we'll be needing any help, thank you." *We?* Well, there was a "we" in her head anyway, even if Merle would have told him she was alone.

"And we don't hire vagrants."

"I didn't know your husband, Ms. Smalls, but I know

Merle. He and my older brother, Jerry, went to high school together. My family has lived here as long as you."

"Then why are you looking for work?" *Men your age looking for a job are just drunks.*

"I had a job putting up fence for the state. But I had to come home to be closer to my family. My mother is sick."

She wavered even as Bud railed in her head, "You gotta be a fool to fall for that, Leah. Get rid of him!"

"Can I fix this gate for you?" He stepped around her and began untangling the wires. "It was too hard for you to close, right?"

Against the ruckus Bud was raising in her head, she said, "I couldn't even open it."

The man hummed while he worked. Wire and staples flew through his hands, and in five minutes, he turned to her and said, "You try to close it now, Ms. Smalls." He held the gate post out to her.

For an instant, both their hands held the gate post. His knuckles were thick and dirt-caked next to her hand, paper-white and pudgy. He let go and the weight of the post pulled at her arm. She grabbed for it with the other hand, hoping he hadn't noticed that she'd nearly dropped it. She didn't want anyone, much less this Mexican, knowing how useless she was. She turned, planted the post in the bottom loop and tugged at the gate. It stretched easily now and she slipped the top loop over it.

"Better, huh?"

It chafed that she'd become beholden to him. "I owe you something for doing that. What's your name, anyway?"

"Julian. Julian Elasario Ruiz."

She paused to listen to Bud. "What the heck kinda name is that?"

"You come on back to the house and I'll pay you for the gate."

He followed her down the dirt track. The putt-a-putt-putt of the motorcycle behind the pickup grated on her nerves.

Every time she accelerated to put some distance between them, she hit a rock in the trail. Pepper, curled on the floor, grunted at the jolts. A hot wind blew through the cab.

She glanced back at him in her rear view mirror, then gazed at herself. Stray gray hairs fell over her forehead. She frowned at the creases around her mouth, the flabby skin on her jowls. A wonder he hadn't looked at her and run. Sooner she got rid of him the better.

She hit another rock, tossing Pepper in the air.

"C'mon up here, honey," she said. She reached for the back of the dog's neck and hauled her onto the seat. *Another affront to the dearly departed.* Bud never allowed dogs on his pickup seat. Pepper scooted onto her lap and huffed more hot air in her face.

Julian passed her to open the last gate into the yard. As she drove through, she called out, "You wait here. I'm going to the house to get you some money."

She tore through her kitchen and into the study, searching for her wallet. How much to pay him that wouldn't be an insult? He'd driven all the way out here. But she hadn't asked him to come, that was his own fool choice. Ten dollars, twenty dollars? She glanced out at the window.

He stood leaning against the truck. Pepper waddled up to him and he squatted and rubbed the thick ruff around her neck.

If she turned him away, would someone else come? One of the ranch boys? Even as the sun scorched the range from dawn until dusk, the days were shortening. Fall was coming. Another three and a half months, snow would be on the ground.

She had to hire this man.

She dropped the wallet on her desk and went back out.

Julian straightened. He was waiting for her to speak, and yet she didn't know how to steer the exchange, how to take command. And here he was, awaiting direction.

"I've changed my mind," she blurted. "You'll have to stay in the bunkhouse. It hasn't been cleaned in years. Room'll be part of your pay, just like it is everywhere else. And food, I'll provide that. I'm not cooking, understand. There's a hot plate in the bunkhouse. No days off during haying, except for rain days. If you've told the truth about living around here, you know that."

He nodded.

"And another thing. There'll be no lock on your door. I can come in whenever I like to make sure you don't have liquor. Or drugs. Got that?"

"Yes, I got it."

"Let's get you set up then." That's it, she'd struck the right tone. This was a favor to him. She didn't have to show any gratitude.

She threw her shoulders back and marched to the bunkhouse, confident that Julian was trailing behind. The sight of the porch planks split and rotting at ground level just made her jut her chin a little higher. Until she noticed whole sections of shingles missing from the roof. Never mind. He wasn't staying for winter. Haying was only a month, month-and-a-half. This bunkhouse was plenty good for that purpose.

The door scraped on the floor as she tried to open it. She looked back at Julian as if this was always the way the door behaved — not to worry. She bumped it with her shoulder, but it only opened another few inches before it jammed against something on the other side. When was the last time she'd been in here? She sucked in her stomach and squeezed through the opening.

Then she gasped at what faced her.

The refrigerator that had given out ten years earlier blocked the door. Other junk that Bud had been too lazy to haul away clogged the room: oil drums, used cattle vaccine bottles, rusted mattress springs, pop cans. Playboy magazines, sprinkled with mouse droppings, were scattered on the bed.

That bastard. He'd done it deliberately. He'd escaped, knowing that he'd left this heap of rot for her to find. He'd have known she'd see this and surrender to his brothers. She could see them back at her kitchen table, their heads nodding like bobblehead dolls. *It's too much for ya, Leah.*

Julian poked his head around the door. The pretense of authority she'd conjured up to govern him had been ripped, revealing her for what she was: a fat, quaking widow.

Julian released a long sigh through his teeth.

"No one's been here in a long time," he offered, as if he was apologizing.

"Bud and I..." Her voice crackled. She would not break down in front of him. She would reassert herself.

"Bud and I — we haven't had ranch hands in a long time. My nephews, Grady and Merle's boys, they help us out now that they're grown. They used to help us out...help me out. I never thought..." In spite of herself, a sob bubbled at the back of her throat. "I needed hay help. I didn't know that I didn't have a place for anyone to stay."

She expected Julian to bolt. She anticipated the sound of his steps on the floorboards and the motorcycle roaring to life. But all she heard was his breathing as he lingered in the doorway.

"I'll get this cleaned up," she said. "I can get it done while you get your things."

"I will help you."

Throughout the stifling afternoon, they hauled trash out of the bunkhouse, loaded it in Bud's pickup, swept, scrubbed, mopped. By evening, the room was habitable. They hauled over the mattress from her guest room, and she rounded up spare soup cans from her pantry. She threw out the fly-spotted curtains, washed the set from her own laundry room and hung them for him. White five-and dime curtains with lavender and lime-colored flowers. Not exactly manly, but Julian didn't seem to mind. He thanked her and said goodnight.

Before Leah went to bed, she looked out her kitchen window. The light shone through the curtains, outlining the shapes of the ridiculous flowers. She thought of him yanking off his undershirt and stirring the chili on his hot plate.

He'd likely snuck some of those Playboys from the trash. He could be thumbing through them, even now.

A jumble of feelings agitated inside her: relief, but also a kind of wonder that just yards away, another life moved in tandem with hers. Under these journeying stars, two lights burned at the Bud Smalls ranch.

III

Julian's rap on the door soon became familiar. When she didn't answer, he'd rap harder and call, "Ms. Smalls?" Only then would she poke her head out, or inch out onto the porch, pulling the door shut behind her. He wasn't allowed inside. Bud would have loathed him.

Once Julian pried her from her lair, he'd report some problem and she'd nod her head like she understood what he was talking about. Most of the time, the result of these exchanges was a trip to the auto parts store where she'd wait in line with other ranchers or their wives. Bud's death was still fresh enough in their minds that they'd jump-start the small talk with, "Sorry about Bud," "What a shock," or "How you holding up, Leah?" If she didn't hustle them on with questions about their own families, they'd leap-frog to the question she dreaded the most: "How are you getting along with Grady and Merle?"

The telephone wires had to be abuzz these days with gossip about the Smalls family. Anything she could say would only fuel it. She didn't want her life dissected. She didn't want anyone's pity. On the other hand, if she answered that it was none of their business, they'd call her a bitch. So she would stiffen and chirp, "Fine, just fine."

After delivering Julian's machine parts to the hayfield, she'd drive home and pour herself a glass of iced tea. She'd dragged out an old thousand-piece puzzle from her closet, a headshot of Elvis. Hour after hour, she fitted Elvis' jacket sequins together while the table fan swirled hot air around the kitchen. Nights, she'd look up from her dishwater to the light in the bunkhouse. It became a game to picture Julian's small routines pieced together from items she'd picked up for him in town: shaving cream, nail clippers, laundry detergent, transistor radio, cigarettes, Tony Hillerman novels. And somewhere in there, a stash of *Playboys*. No matter. His putterings about the ranch insulated her from sun, wind, failure.

Knock, knock, knock.

"Ms. Smalls?" he called for the third time.

Leah stepped out into the searing sunlight. "What is it?"

"Are you well?"

She shaded her eyes. "I am well, thank you."

"Then, I have to ask, why you are not out here putting up hay."

She fumed. "It's what I hired you to do."

He glanced at his boots, then looked up at her again.

"Have you thought how long it will take? If I am the only one mowing and baling this hay? It might take until Columbus Day. We might be knee-deep in snow."

"Bud always managed."

"You said his brothers and their sons helped, right? Are they coming now?"

"I don't think so. No."

"You've never raked hay? Or baled?"

"I was never expected to be out there," she snapped. She ticked off all the things she couldn't say: *I was never wanted out there, I couldn't have done anything to suit them out there.*

"You gonna hire some more help?"

She considered the money left in the ranch account. And what she was paying Julian. And the bills: auto parts store, ranch supply store, hardware store.

"What do you want me to do?"

He waited while she changed clothes. She put on a pair of jeans and then thumbed through Bud's shirts. Shirt after shirt was faded, worn, stained. It didn't make sense, but she wanted to look good.

At last, she picked one of his dress shirts — well, not like he was going out to dinner anymore — a blue and white striped one with abalone snaps. The material had a nice sheen to it. She put it on and looked at herself in the mirror. Not bad. Then she put on her wide-brimmed straw hat. She hated caps. And cowboy hats always blew off. She tightened the string under her chin. *There.* Now she looked like a respectable rancher's wife. Off to the hayfields.

From outside, Julian was warbling *Your Cheatin' Heart*, but he stopped abruptly once she stepped out the door. How foolish to expect him to say how nice she looked. *It's business.* This is what a business relationship is about, she thought. Besides, she was old enough to be his mother — well, if she'd gotten pregnant in high school. That was unspeakable in those days, pregnancy. One or two girls — always the ones her mother had warned about, the ones who'd draped themselves on boys' cars — were plucked from the class and vanished, as if the earth had opened up and swallowed them whole. She wondered how old Julian's mother was.

"How's your mother, Julian?" she asked.

Julian nodded his appreciation. "She had chemo in Cheyenne. She's home now. She's doing better."

Teenage sex to chemo. Fast as a speeding bullet.

Julian hummed Hank Williams tunes under his breath while he drove to the hayfield. She rested her arm on the open window and watched the meadowlarks flutter up as they passed. Riding with Bud, the view from the window had always been framed by his grumbles about the "boys," the livestock, the machinery, the weather. Now, no more rants to listen to.

She inhaled the smell of fresh cut grass.

Julian pulled up in front of the hay rake. "Have you driven a tractor before?"

"Of course," she snorted.

"But you haven't raked hay."

"No."

"Then I will show you. First you will need to grease the machine."

"I need to do what?"

"OK. I will grease it. Can you check the oil in the tractor?"

It hardly seemed fair for her to stand around while he did all the work on the machinery. She might be his boss, but she wasn't the Queen of England.

"I'll check the oil."

Now he launched into *Hey Good Lookin'*. He grabbed the grease gun and flitted about the machine.

The tractor needed oil. Leah was almost pleased; she could show him that she could be of use. She hauled out the oil container from the pickup bed, poured it into a beaker and filled the tractor. When she'd put everything back, she looked down. Bud's blue-striped dress shirt was smeared in grease and oil.

Julian looked up at her squawking.

"I wondered, Ms. Smalls, why you wore that nice shirt to come out here." And he went back to greasing.

She could race back to the house, rip the shirt off, slather on the stain remover and be back here in just a minute. Julian could wait—of course he would wait, he was her employee, after all.

"OK, we're ready. Can you get on the tractor now?" he asked.

"I need to change shirts."

Julian shifted his weight from one foot to the other, the same way Bud used to do whenever he was annoyed with her. She pictured Bud superimposed over Julian.

"Damn it, Leah!" Julian's befuddled features replaced Bud's as the image dissipated.

"Why do you need to change shirts?"

"I'm covered in grease!" She sounded ridiculous, even to herself.

"OK. You can go and change shirts. If you like. But there is no one out here to look at you. There is no one out here to notice a little grease. Maybe you can leave it today. Then, maybe tomorrow, you can bring out two shirts? One to wear, and a spare?"

He was so deferential. She hated him for it. If he'd just stomp around and shout, like Bud, she could snap back. Now, any course of action, other than following his suggestion, looked silly.

"I guess I'll have to leave it. If you say so."

Julian grinned and said, "OK. You can rake now, right?"

She drove the tractor while he stood behind her and yammered instructions.

"Now Ms. Smalls, you see this lever here on your right? You need to set it down, no, not hard, slow, slow, there you go, now see, the rake lowers, flips the hay. See you are doing it, you are raking hay."

He was leaning over her and his breath in her ear unsettled her. Wafts of his *Old Spice* aftershave mingled with the exhaust blasting back from the tractor's smokestack. Leah wanted to scoot away from him, but instead she clenched the wheel. After a few minutes, he straightened, and while she was relieved, she felt conscious of his hands gripping the seat. She stiffened her spine to make sure there was no contact between them, to let him know there would be no relaxation of formality.

"OK, Ms. Smalls, I see you're good now. I am going to mow some more." She stopped and watched him stride over the rows of mown hay, the grass swishing around his boots. The sun bore down, burning off the last cool breeze.

She heard, "*So if you want to have fun, come along with me*" before the mower roared to life and jerked forward, chewing into the long grass.

For the first hour, she was caught up in the work, attentive to every detail of her machine. But as it became rote, the heat oppressed her. The tractor's rumble reverberated in her brain. *Come to think of it, Bud always brought a transistor radio out here.* She'd have to dig around in his drawers for it when she got home.

Two hours, three hours. *So this was what it's like to sit on a tractor all day. Hot, boring.* Couldn't she find some excuse to leave? She stopped to sip from her canteen. The water was lukewarm, metallic-tasting. Beyond her, Julian's mower chugged along, grass falling in its wake.

At noon, they stopped at a reservoir. As her tractor engine puttered out, the silence flooded her senses, sweeping all her thoughts from her head. Above, the windmill blades twirled lazily. *God, I can still see Bud up there tinkering with that thing.* At each revolution, the windmill creaked. *Gone, gone, gone.*

Julian ripped off his teeshirt and dove into the water. He splashed around, then stood up, filled the crown of his straw hat and poured it over his head. Water streamed down his torso and his jeans clung to him, sodden.

She watched in a stupor.

Children are allowed to behave that way, not men. A man might complain about the heat. He might take his handkerchief and mop his head. He might dip some water in his hands and throw it on his face. But men do not indulge themselves, not the Smalls brothers, anyway.

Julian waded out and wiped his face on his teeshirt.

"You're not hot, Ms. Smalls?"

"No." She hesitated. "I am hot, but that won't make me go skinny-dipping."

"It's wrong? To take a swim?"

She didn't answer.

She unfolded the wax paper from her tuna sandwich. Julian collapsed in the shade of the pickup. He opened a can of beef stew and spooned it down in great heaps. Pepper crept next to him with her ears perked, silently begging for a spoonful. She was rewarded with the dribbles that fell from his spoon.

Leah looked off to where the muddy water sloshed, sunlight glinting off the waves.

"Where does your family live, Julian?"

"You know the railroad stop, Angel Ledge?"

She knew the place. It was off the highway north of Thistle — a couple of collapsed sheds, the sign, and beyond that, a ridge dotted with greasewood. A little trail meandered over the railroad tracks and on up the ridge. The quaint name had always made her smile. She imagined an angel flitting on the rotting platform, only to be shredded by the wind.

"Yes."

"That road over the railroad tracks…"

"That's a road? It never looked like anything more than a sheep trail."

He paused at her interruption. "Maybe you never noticed. It's a road. It goes up the ridge to my parents' house on top. There's a windbreak around the house. You've never seen that?"

Vaguely, she did remember a plank windbreak on the top. She'd assumed it was just another crumbling remnant connected with the station.

"My dad — he's got two sections there. We got a little hay meadow along the Angel Ditch, and we run eighty head of cattle. My brother Jerry, the one that knows your brother-in-law, he's running the place now."

How did a family of Mexicans acquire a ranch? Never mind that it was a small one. All the Mexicans she'd seen worked for other people. She'd certainly never seen brown-skinned folks at the Hatton County Stockgrowers' Association meetings! *Would that even have been allowed?*

She tried to make her voice as neutral as possible. "How did your family get the ranch?"

Julian scraped the bottom of the can. Pepper had given up on any more drips and dropped down next to him with a grunt. Julian scraped and scraped, as if the answer to Leah's question was somehow stuck to the bottom of the can. He took one more lick off his spoon and then his arm dropped to his knee.

"We worked. My dad drove trucks up and down this country until he had enough money to buy a ranch in foreclosure. The guy that lost it…" he gestured toward her with his spoon, "…he was a white guy."

He set the can down and Pepper took it between her paws. Julian leaned back against the truck tire and closed his eyes.

The white bread gummed up in Leah's mouth. Water — her mouth was too dry — that was it. She took another swig from her canteen. The water had become so hot that she nearly spat it out. No, she couldn't do something that rude in front of him. Instead, she swallowed it fast and nearly choked.

Julian opened his eyes. "Are you all right, Ms. Smalls?"

Leah looked for a napkin to wipe her mouth, then remembered she hadn't brought any. Julian tossed over his handkerchief and it landed in her lap. She wavered between not wanting to touch it and the thought of offending him if she didn't. He was the ranch hand for God's sake — she shouldn't care what he thought.

She stared at it before picking it up by the corner and gingerly patting her mouth.

Julian smiled. "Better?"

She nodded and held it out to him. As he took it back, the look in his eyes made her squirm. He'd seen through her, read her prejudice. *What does he know?* She wasn't prejudiced. She made a show of wiping crumbs off her thighs.

"Your nephew, Merle, Jr., that's Merle's son, right? I seen him at Foster's gas station about a month ago. He pushed ahead of me in the checkout line. He had a big smirk on his face."

That story was no exaggeration. She imagined Merle, Jr. and the rest of her nephews — six of them. The last time she'd seen them was at branding: popping the lids off their beer cans, spitting their chew, pawing their girlfriends. She knew exactly how any one of them would behave in front of Julian. Not long ago, she would never have given it a second thought. Now she imagined the pinch of wearing Julian's shoes.

"I'm sorry," she said.

Julian jumped to his feet. "We got to get back to work, Ms. Smalls."

She envied how easily he moved, while she couldn't push herself off the ground. Nine-hundred pound cows struggled less to get to their feet.

Julian reached out his hand.

She looked up at him. The sun, just past its zenith, was too glaring for her to make out his features. But she didn't hesitate this time. She gripped his hand and he pulled her to her feet.

It was dusk when they returned home, both of them sweat-caked and greasy. Leah was so tired that she'd forgotten all about Bud's blue-striped dress shirt that was now not only grease-stained, but covered in brown soot and dirt.

Julian leaned against the hood and pushed his hat back on his head. "Tomorrow?"

"Yes, Julian, I'll be out in the morning."

"Good night, Ms. Smalls."

Inside, she peeled off Bud's shirt and her jeans and put them in the washing machine to soak. She padded to her bedroom in her underwear and pulled out a housecoat, a flower and striped affair she'd bought more than twenty years ago.

She stumbled back out to the kitchen, switched on the light and thought about supper. A can of tomato soup, that's all she had the energy to fix. She slurped it down, rinsed the pot. Outside, Julian's light burned. What had he eaten? She thought of the huge meals she used to fix for Bud during haying: platters of fried chicken, gallon bowls of mashed potatoes, jello salads. She could have at least made Julian a jello salad.

IV

After the hay was baled and stacked, the ranch eased into the dwindling summer. Skies overhead were cloudless, and though patches of the meadows had been blanched by frost, large swaths of green remained. No more birdsong in the mornings, but cattails sprang from the irrigation ditches. As Leah gathered them, grasshoppers buzzed along the banks She set the cattails in a large vase in her living room, where they'd always been, autumn after autumn. In the late afternoons, their shadows fell across Bud's recliner, patched here and there with duct tape.

As she'd watched Julian stack the last bales, she realized there was no sense in letting him go, now that fall round-up and shipping were right around the corner. He took up the fall tasks Bud used to do, cleaning ditches and repairing fence. He could manage these things without her, just as Bud had, so the daily rapping on her door stopped. She waved to him from the kitchen window.

Leah decided that the time has come to return to the monthly meetings of her women's group, the Chuck-Wagon Gals. When she'd spotted a few of the Gals on her trips to town, they always asked when she would be coming back. A respectable period of mourning had passed. It was time for her grand re-entry.

Leah had never enjoyed a Chuck-Wagon Gal program. *How many ways can a person present cocktail weenies?* But she liked the Gals, themselves. Oh, there were a few who were excruciatingly gung-ho about the ranching enterprise. They yakked on and on about their adventures alongside their men, but there were also those, like her, who craved a discussion of something other than cows.

Leah was the first to pull into the Rams Inn parking lot, where the meetings were held. After she pushed out of the driver's seat, she lifted her face to the sun. As she felt the warmth against her closed eyelids, she fretted over how fleeting it was. One more month and Thistle's streets would be striped with ridges of ice that wouldn't melt until March.

"Leah, is that you?"

Leah opened her eyes to see Ginny Feister a few spaces away. Ginny was a good ten years younger. Her purse was always stuffed with pictures of children that Leah couldn't tell apart. *"Now that's Spencer, right?" "No, that's Tressy."*

Nothing, not even the wheel of ranch plagues—fire, flood, drought and cattle disease—ever dented Ginny's exuberance. Over the years, Leah had come to dread the cheery lilt in her voice. Get over it, she'd wanted to say. The decades, bearing down on Ginny sure as eighteen-wheelers, would squash her flat, just as they had Leah.

"Oh, honey, how are you?" Ginny threw her arms around Leah and hugged her tight. Despite how she'd thought of Ginny, tears burned in Leah's eyes. She pulled away. Hadn't she toughened up over the last four months? She hadn't come here to blubber.

"I'm fine, really I am."

Ginny gripped her by the shoulders. "Why have you been away so long? We've missed you!"

Leah dabbed at her eyes. "I was just overwhelmed by it all. It was such a shock — Bud there one day and gone the next."

Ginny nodded sympathetically.

"And then that ranch. I'm not like you, Ginny. I've never done any of the outdoor work. It wasn't until I hired someone that I had to get out there and..." She hesitated. By now, the whole Chuck-Wagon Gal nation knew a Mexican was living on her place.

Ginny turned at the sound of other cars arriving. Chuck-Wagon Gals emerged, their voices bubbly with greetings. Some of the women hadn't been to town in a month, and in their voices Leah could hear the relief at release from isolation.

The wave of women slowly funneled into the motel dining room, and in the doorway, she ran smack into Merle's wife, Darcy.

Darcy squeezed her wrist. "Leah, what a stranger you've been!"

Leah stared into the brown eyes of a woman she remembered as a girl, eyes now sunk like buttons in a sallow pancake face. Year after year, she'd complimented Darcy's home perms, oohed and ahhed over her desiccated Thanksgiving turkeys. She'd attended every baptism, brought a trunk-full of gifts every Christmas. After Darcy's hysterectomy, she'd stayed with her for ten days, done her cooking and cleaning. Yet Darcy was right. She had turned into a stranger.

"It's not exactly the same now, is it?"

Just a smidgen of sympathy tweaked the corners of Darcy's mouth.

"I should have called you, Leah. Merle and Grady — they're trying to do what's best for you. Don't you see that? You don't want to be running that ranch on your own. Come over and talk to them. I'll help you."

She smiled, so confident that Leah would accept her invitation. She was right. The Leah Smalls Darcy used to know would have gladly trooped over and let everyone else decide.

"Hon, the ham and scalloped potato casserole you brought over after the funeral was divine, it really was. But, I don't need any help right now."

Leah found a seat in between Ginny and Lorena Castle, an odd pairing. Lorena was every bit as dour as Ginny was peppy. She acknowledged Leah's presence with the barest twitch of her eyebrows.

The program was on quilting wall calendars. "Easy-to-make Christmas presents for those extras on your list," explained the presenter, a Mrs. Alice Meisler, the extension agent's wife who'd driven all the way down from Casper. Everyone clapped loudly when she'd finished, and some of the more raucous Gals hooted their approval.

When the salads were served, Ginny and Lorena turned to her. Leah couldn't hope to lag in the conversation and murmur at everyone else's anecdotes. What with all the talk that would have circulated in her absence, she knew she was the main course. *Leap into the breach, that was the way to go.*

"I know you two wouldn't have believed it when Bud passed, but I'm managing so far. I've got the hay up."

Lorena stared at her. "You didn't get it done by yourself. Darcy says you hired a Mexican."

Ginny's fork paused in mid-air. "You hired someone? I thought Grady and Merle's boys were helping you."

Oh God, she really hasn't heard. How can that be? And there's Lorena, her lips pooched forward like a vulture's beak.

All these years Leah had reveled in family dramas, along with the rest of the Gals. Weren't the programs — cocktail weenies, quilted wall calendars, painted antelope skulls, and so forth — just a cover for rooting in one another's closets?

With a glance at Lorena, she said, "Bud's death was so unexpected and all, right before haying. All of them were tied up. You know Merle, Jr. got married, don't you? It wouldn't have been right, asking those boys to drop the summer jobs they'd already lined up."

"You better watch that Ruiz boy," said Lorena, "That's what Darcy says. She says Merle only sent him over there because he knew you couldn't get by on your own. But Darcy says he, or his relatives, will rob you blind one of these days, if he hasn't already. Have you checked your equipment lately? He could've taken half the parts for the machinery and you'd never know it."

Leah sat, stupefied. No, she had not been out to the equipment shed since haying ended. She recalled how patient Julian always was with her. Was it a ruse? Would he steal her blind? Was he doing that right now?

"It's so easy for the two of you! You've got husbands and children. I wish you could have been me for just one day. I wish you could have stepped out your doors and seen it all staring you in the face, with no one there and no one coming. The two of you couldn't do it all by yourselves, any better than me."

She stabbed a radish. "It's not like Julian is a foreigner. He's one of us. His family has a place right there at the old Angel Ledge station."

"There's nothing out there but a junk pile," said Lorena."You're being lied to."

"Leah, honey," said Ginny, "I think you need to go talk to Grady and Merle. You shouldn't be so proud. They'll help you."

Ginny and Lorena's faces lingered in Leah's mind as she floored it up the highway. Over the miles, their voices subsided to whispers, and by the time she turned off the highway, she was alone again. No presences, only her purse on the seat beside her. She paused at the iron arch Bud had welded over their entrance: *Bud Smalls Ranch.*

When Bud was alive, it rankled that the arch excluded her name. But now, as she looked through her dust-caked windshield, the idea of trumpeting a claim over acres of sagebrush seemed absurd. These sprawling ranches that whipped families into such a furor were more conceptual than real.

The last sunbeams bored through the clouds on the horizon, shooting orange streaks deep into the sky. In the distance, Bud's buildings and corrals, puny as a child's blocks, squatted at the edge of the oncoming dark.

The pickup was parked down the fence line. Julian's windbreaker flapped in the wind as he tightened wire. He waved. She half-lifted her hand, then dropped it. He might see it as an invitation to come over, ask her how her luncheon had been. How could she respond without him detecting the suspicions that had been planted in her mind?

She floored it toward the house.

Pepper thumped her tail on the porch as Leah got out of the car. The dog stood up, expecting a pat on the head, but Leah ignored her and headed to the equipment shed. She rolled open the heavy door. The haying machinery was neatly parked. The odors—gas and cured hay—brought back the haying season, and she remembered dragging herself to the pickup at sunset each day while Julian kept on working until dark. She opened drawers one by one to see tools neatly stacked and cleaned. She rummaged among the cabinets. Nails had been sorted into tin cans. Layers of dead flies that Bud always ignored had been cleaned off shelves. The floor was swept clean.

After she'd heaved the door shut, she thought of the bunkhouse. The floorboards creaked as she approached the door, little squeaks of the guilt she was suppressing. Her hand rested on the doorknob. Well, she had warned him, hadn't she?

She shouldered the door open. The room smelled

musty though a whiff of his *Old Spice* remained. Looking at his rumpled sheets, his nightstand with wallet and coins, his laundry mounded on the floor, she felt as if she was looking at him naked. Who was the pilferer, now?

The truck rumbled in the yard and her heart jolted. She quickly shut the door and tried to mold herself into the shadows. The dusk had thickened, and in the yard light, Julian sang *Lovesick Blues* as he opened the tailgate to unload the posts and wire. She thought she could sneak off the porch, but the floorboards gave her away.

"Leah?"

She stepped under the light, unable to pretend she'd been on some other errand.

"It's me."

"Can I help you with something?"

"I was checking your room. I told you I'd be doing that from time to time."

She braced for the hurt. Or anger.

"Are you sure you saw everything? Because if you didn't, you know, you should go back, check some more."

"No. Everything's fine, thank you." She turned her back on him, intending to project an unruffled dignity, but she felt as if she was scuttling from his presence.

"It's OK. I must sweep the truck out," he called after her.

Back in her kitchen, she watched the indigo sky deepen to black. Moments ticked by and still she stood there in the dark. The Milky Way rippled down the sky, oblivious to the voices in her head, as it followed its own currents to the end of time.

She went to the door and reached for Bud's jacket that hung from a peg. The night air, already chilled with the winter to come, whooshed in her face.

Julian opened the door a crack after she knocked. Leah searched his face for the emotion that she knew had to be there. She riffled through her justifications, preparing for his accusation, but he remained slumped against the door jamb and the silence grew awkward.

"I went to my meeting in town today…"

"The Cattle Ladies, right?"

"Chuck-Wagon Gals. They just wanted me to watch out for myself. That's all."

"You don't have to apologize, Ms. Smalls. It's your ranch. I am just here for a little while. When my mother gets well, I'm going to leave. So it doesn't matter."

Such stoniness in his eyes. He had never looked that way before.

"I wished you'd told me that you'd cleaned up that old machine shed. And all the tools. If Bud came back, he wouldn't recognize it."

"I did tell you. One morning, I knocked and you didn't answer. I opened the door and called inside. You wouldn't come out of your kitchen. You said you were busy."

Busy. Working on Elvis' pompadour.

"I've made a mistake. I'm sorry, Julian."

His mouth relaxed, but he said nothing more. She fumbled for the words that would wipe out this uneasiness between them. *Please God, I don't want it to be this way when he shuts that door.*

"Is there anything else?" Julian asked.

Yes. No. She shook her head.

"Good night, Ms. Smalls."

The door latch clicked in place. Inside, she heard Buck Owens on the transistor radio, "*Together – again…*" Strains of dobro trailed her back to her kitchen.

Ⅴ

The Goodyear Blimp, that's what she looked like in Bud's thermal underwear and coveralls. Womens' fashion had yet to make it here to the high plains. As she knotted her neck scarf, she imagined the hellcat wind ripping the fur hats from those TV models.

Any minute now, Julian would knock, though it was still dark outside. Shipping day. Judgment day, really. This was the day she'd find out whether she'd make enough income to support this place.

The furnace rattled and coughed, drowning out the sound of wind. *Please Lord, not a blizzard today.*

There it was, the soft rapping. The doorknob was so cold to the touch that she paused to button the collar on Bud's coveralls. Sure enough, when she opened the door, the blast of cold took her breath away. Scattered hard snowflakes bounced about the yard.

Julian wore only that same greasy windbreaker over a hooded sweatshirt.

"I saddled your horse, Ms. Smalls."

"Julian, you'll freeze to death!"

"Don't worry, I'll be all right." His hood was pulled tight around his head, almost down to his eyebrows.

As they gathered the calves, the dark receded, revealing a dense grey sky. Just another thing to worry about—what this storm might do—on top of how much her calves would weigh and how she would square up to the Smalls brothers.

Merle had grudgingly agreed to let her use the scales in his corrals for shipping. Just before she'd hung up the phone, he'd blurted, "You still got that Mexican?"

Sonofabitch. Of course, he knew. He and Grady had been spying on her for months. She'd watched their pickups trolling the fence lines, rolling to a stop every so often. No doubt that's when they'd whip out their binoculars and zoom in on whatever piqued them.

"I thought you kept up with what's going on here."

"Been outta touch this last week or so."

"He's working out just fine. Thank you for sending him."

Merle paused. "We'll have a long winter. I hear his mama's not doing too well. Once she's gone, he's got nothing to hold him. By calving season, you could be high and dry, with no help. You let us know if that happens."

"And you'll come?"

"I'm thinking our offer will look a lot better to you when you're calving two hundred cows by yourself."

God, I'd love to tell him to screw his damn scales.

This morning it was *Jambalaya* Julian belted out as he hustled the lead calves up the road, slapping Bud's rope against the saddle. The ice pellets blowing in Leah's face reminded her of that hail storm she'd been trapped in with Bud all those years ago. That howling she'd done back then—it hadn't come from her physical misery alone. No, what had fueled her rage at Bud that day was her sense of injustice at being in a place where she didn't have to be. She'd thought she had a choice to ride away and leave the mess to him. She had been comfortable after all, never having to commit herself.

"Son of a gun, we're having fun on the Range-o."

Even as her fingers froze around the reins, the twist in the words made her smile. Where Bud would be spitting curses, Julian would sing. In the past few weeks, when Julian hadn't been watching, her grip on convention had buckled and she'd found herself humming along.

When she'd fingered a puzzle piece the morning after the Chuck-Wagon Gals meeting, she'd looked into Elvis' eyes and seen Julian's. They bored into her head, challenging her indifference. She argued back. *You weren't here all these years listening to 'the boys', you didn't see how I got crowded out.* Jigsaw Julian wore the same stony expression that the real Julian had that night at the bunkhouse. Capable or not, he expected her to be out there, to recognize his efforts if nothing else.

Did she want to keep her ranch hand?

Out went the Elvis puzzle. On went the coveralls.

It was no use. She couldn't hold the reins any more. She dismounted and walked behind the calves, their hoofbeats *ratta-tat-tatting* on the frozen road.

Julian sang all the way to the corrals. Through the haze, she saw Grady and Merle waiting at the gate. They must have heard him long before they saw him. With their hoods on, she couldn't see their reaction as the calves filed into the pens. Julian leaned from his horse and shook their hands. As she came through, Merle, Jr. closed the gate behind her.

"It's been a long time, Aunt Leah. How ya been?" He jerked his thumb in Julian's direction. "You know, I could find you some better help. Remember Cousin Ray? He's back in town."

"From the army. I heard. He got a dishonorable discharge, right?"

Calves suddenly sprinted up the alley, churning up muck on her coveralls, and she heard Julian shout.

"What's going on?"

"Uh, sorry Aunt Leah, looks like we forgot to close the gate at the other end. Your calves are going back out into ours."

Leah scrambled up the fence to see. Julian spurred his horse for the open gate to cut off the escaping calves. The horse jumped into the gap and calves wheeled back, but more than fifty were already gone, charging into Merle's cattle.

Bud's curses were so loud in her ears that she thought they'd split her skull.

"Sorry about that, Leah," said Merle grimly, as he walked up to her. Grady stood with his hands in his pockets, watching Julian shut the gate.

"Merle Smalls, you've never left a gate open! When I think of the times you've shouted at me for not closing gates!"

Grady leaned over and spat his chew. "Now just quit your ragging. You know it was an accident. Merle wouldn'ta done this on purpose."

"Wouldn't he? Aren't all these calves standing here, no food, no water, losing weight every minute while we try to fix this?"

Merle, Jr. joined them. "Dad, the trucks are here."

"Damnit, son. Didn't I tell you to check these corrals before breakfast this morning?"

"No, you told Shaun to do it."

Sure enough, two semis were rolling up to the corrals. Beyond, in Merle's pasture, Julian rode at a full gallop, struggling to gather her herd on his own.

Merle turned to Leah. "You're forgetting that you're using these scales for free. Now we'll send Julian back to help you load the calves that are right here. That won't cost you a penny. We'll gather the rest.

"Junior, go on out there and send Julian back." Merle

started toward his horse. He looked back over his shoulder. "If you ever want our help again, Leah, you'd better be ready to apologize when I get back."

The buyer arrived and introduced himself as they rode out.

"Sorry to hear about your husband, Ms. Smalls. Bud was a true cattleman, one of the best." He glanced at the calves standing in the alley and the idling trucks. "What are we waiting for?"

Leah tried to curb her anger. "Some of the calves got away. My brothers-in-law went to get them."

Julian slogged back through the muck in the alley. His face was seared from windburn and his horse heaved.

"I can push the calves that are here onto the scales — the truck drivers, they will help."

"I'll help you. They're my cattle. *Our* cattle."

She glanced nervously at the buyer. *Our cattle?*

She'd meant the Smalls cattle, hers and Bud's, of course. She started to correct herself, but both men had already left her standing there. Julian was pushing calves down the alley, and the buyer held the gate open.

He called to her. "You'll want to come with me and check these weights, won't you?"

In the time it took for the Smalls to round up their cattle and sort out her calves, Leah's fingers and toes turned numb with cold. At first, she tried jumping up and down to keep her feet warm, but her energy shriveled in the driving wind. Merle didn't speak to her again. *Just as well.* She'd have gladly frozen to death before she'd spit out some kind of apology. The last she saw them, they were riding up the road to Merle's.

Sonsofbitches. How many meals had Bud missed when he'd gone running to help them?

Once the last bunch of calves were swept onto the trucks, the buyer offered to let her sit in his car. Her teeth chattered even as the fan blasted hot air. Through the windshield wipers, she barely made out Julian mounting his horse and leading hers out of the corral.

"I'll take you for coffee," the buyer offered, "We'll get you warmed up."

The kitchen was already sunk in gloom when he brought her home, what with the short November day and the snow piling against the house. She switched on the overhead light, brewed more coffee and cranked up that caterwauling furnace. She couldn't get warm. She ran a scalding bath, and even in the tub, her teeth chattered. Once she'd dried, she wrapped herself in two bathrobes, and collapsed into her chair at the kitchen table.

There was the check, a year's labor, a year begun with Bud and ending with her. She smoothed it over until it lay flat. She'd barely glimpsed these checks over the years as Bud had pocketed them. There, corralled on this strip of paper, was someone else's measure of the sunrise to sunset hours they'd invested through the four seasons. *It amounts to this.*

And with it, she could buy the extension of those days on and on, just as Bud used to do. On sales days, they'd hopped into the car, and Bud had floored it to town. After he paid up all the accounts, he'd take her to dinner. Over the beer and steaks, they'd never spoken of an ending point. They'd never considered it. You just went on. *Until...*

She pulled her bathrobes closer about her neck and looked outside. Only the outlines of buildings were still visible now. The yard light snapped on, and in its eye, the snow swirled in eddies of wind. Beyond the buildings, the corrals, Bud's ranch extended into darkness, settling under layers of snow. *No. Her ranch.* Out in the dark, her cattle bunched with the snow lining their backs.

Julian's light was on. She remembered how chilled she'd

been and thought of his flimsy windbreaker. The electric heater in that bunkhouse couldn't be keeping him warm enough. Yet throughout the fall, he hadn't complained.

Was it right, what she put him through, just so she could stand her ground?

She dressed and pulled on Bud's elk-head sweater. She looked out the window again at the light glowing behind the garish flowers on those silly curtains. Contrary voices — telling her to go, telling her to stay — squawked in her head, raucous as her chickens.

"I'm going," she said aloud.

She pulled on boots and stepped outside. This time, the draft felt refreshing against her cheeks. She crossed the yard and knocked on his door.

"Julian!"

Her heart beat so loud she was sure he could hear it. Suddenly, she prayed he wouldn't answer. If only he was in the shower, or asleep, so she could sneak back across the yard.

She heard him at the door. Too late, she couldn't bolt. Would she see coldness in his eyes again? No, he just looked surprised. His hair was slicked down on his head and drops of water ran down his jaw.

"Is everything all right?"

"Yes. I just wanted to know…if you got back OK. It was such a horrible day, and the weather's so cold, I felt…well, I'm sorry you had to ride back alone."

"Thank you, Ms. Smalls. I'm fine. Tomorrow, I think we need to move the cows to the hay meadows before the weather gets any worse. What do you think?"

"You're right." She could end this conversation now, she realized. But her boots seemed glued to the floorboards. "Look, there's something I want to ask you."

As he waited, the blood pounded in her ears. She shoved the words up out of her throat.

"You're welcome to come have supper with me. If you want. You don't have to."

"You sure?"

"Yes, I'm sure."

"All right. Let me get a nicer shirt."

She flew back across the yard, pleased that he'd agreed to come and panicked by thoughts of what to fix. She hadn't fixed a meal since—well, since Bud died. She rummaged in her chest freezer, pitched hamburger into the microwave, peeled potatoes and yanked dishes from her cupboards. *Damn, these dishes are all grayed and scratched. How did they get that way?*

Why was she fretting over it? This was the ranch hand. These plates had been good enough for her and Bud. Her vision suddenly split between the way she had always seen her kitchen and the way Julian would see it as he walked in and looked down at those Sears plates—brand new wedding plates some thirty years ago.

There was his knock. *Already.* She dashed to the bathroom and looked in the mirror. She hadn't done anything with her hair.

"Coming!" she called out, loud as she could. She swept her hair back into a bun and tweaked a few strands forward so he wouldn't notice how her forehead was balding. She pressed her hands on both sides of her face. *Make-up.* Why hadn't she thought of it before she'd invited him? *No time now.*

Julian removed his boots in the doorway, then tiptoed into the kitchen, as if he expected to be asked to leave at any moment. His eyes roamed about, taking in the rooster clock, the stained walls, the harvest gold refrigerator.

Shabby, Leah thought, as she followed his gaze, although he'd never utter it.

"Smells good," he said.

"It's all right. You can sit down."

He slid into the chair, looking restive. She bustled about the stove, mashing potatoes, stirring gravy, flipping hamburger patties. At last, she ladled food into serving dishes and set it before him. He didn't move.

"Go ahead, you can eat."

"I'm waiting for you."

She sat down, but didn't pick up her fork. Bud was once again superimposed over Julian. Bud's plate would be mounded by now. He'd have shoveled in fork-loads of food already. He wouldn't be just sitting there, looking at her.

Julian had shaved. With his hair combed and shiny and his dark eyes fixed on her, the context was shifting from what she'd intended. All she'd meant was to do him a kindness, but it had begun to feel as if they were on a first date. He'd worn a new flannel shirt.

"Go ahead," she urged again.

"You first."

"No, I don't go first. Bud goes first. I mean, he always went first."

Julian didn't budge. Leah dished herself a dollop of mashed potatoes and passed them to him. Their awkwardness subsided as they ate.

"This is good."

"Salisbury steak, not anything gourmet."

"You did not have to do it, Ms. Smalls."

"Can you stop calling me that?" Her own words surprised her.

"What should I call you?"

"Well…Leah. That's what everybody calls me."

"You are OK with me calling you Leah?"

She thought back to their first meeting out on the prairie. The woman standing by that gate would never have allowed this Mexican to call her by her first name.

"Yes, I want you to call me Leah."

"Leah, were you happy with what you got for your cattle today?"

She put her fork down. No man had ever asked for

her thoughts before. It had always been Bud's place to show satisfaction—or not. He would trumpet whatever was on his mind, and Grady and Merle would respond in chorus.

"Yes, I was happy. Even with Merle and Grady losing the calves the way they did, we did well. There's enough to get through the winter. Maybe even another year, I hope." She paused. "On our own."

"Why are your brothers-in-law driving around, watching us all the time? Why don't they come help you?"

"They want me to leave. I'm just holding them up. I didn't have children. So I'm useless. They want me to get out of here so they can have this place for their kids."

"What do you want?"

Her eyes started to tear at yet another question she'd never heard.

"This was Bud's 'thing'. And I've been here...well... forever." Her voice started to break, "I can't imagine starting over, being some kind of lady in the movies who goes out and saves African rhinos. That's not going to be me. All I want is... my home. That's all."

"You know you can sell this place, right? And move to someplace warm. Like Arizona, maybe."

Leah burst out laughing. *God, what a maniac I must seem.*

"I'm sorry, it's just that..." She wiped tears away with the back of her hand. "Grady and Merle wanted me to move to Arizona."

Julian leaned forward. "I didn't mean to sound like them."

She waved him away. "You're not hurting my feelings. You're just trying to help."

"I'm not sure I can help you."

"With that money from the sale today, I have a chance to see if I can make it."

"Then maybe I can help you."

"You'll be leaving soon, won't you? When your mother has recovered?"

204

He didn't answer. Had she offended him? He picked up his glass of water and drank. Sweat beaded on her forehead. Hot flash, that would be her explanation, if he noticed.

He set his glass down and folded his hands in his lap. "My mother...I want to believe that she will get better, that one day she'll be the way she was. When I was home last Sunday, my brothers and I—we fixed dinner. She came in the kitchen. We told her to go back to the living room. Sit and rest. But she pulled her wig off and threw it on the floor. It was lying there, you know, like a dead animal. She said, 'You treat me like I'm already dead. You are pushing me under. Get out of my kitchen.' And at first, I thought, OK, it's a good sign. But then while we watched football, I thought, no, she is crying out while the illness pulls her away from us.

"I know it was hard for you that Mr. Smalls died so suddenly, with no warning. You had no time to prepare. But think what it is like to watch someone die in pieces— a horror film in the slowest motion with no end. And you can do nothing."

"Is there anything I can do?"

He shook his head. "I don't mean to upset you. I shouldn't've brought it up. No matter what happens, I will help you through calving. Then we will see where we are."

His eyes were so steady, so earnest. She had an urge to squeeze his hand, only because she could think of no other way to extend comfort. But he'd already risen to his feet. Gently, he picked up the chair and set it back against the table.

"It was very good. Thank you."

Wait, you don't have to go. You can sit. She wanted to run to the freezer, paw through all the desserts. *Wouldn't you like a...?* But he'd already pulled on his coat and the drafts blew in the door.

Her kitchen was oddly empty. Bud, that's what was missing. The presence that had lingered there for months had gone as well, sucked out the door into the frigid night.

Jamie Lisa Forbes

VI

The next night she looked out of the kitchen window, hungry for his company. How would it look, Bud's widow eating meals every night with the ranch hand? She swished her dinner dishes in the soapy water. *No, no, there'd be no end to the gossip, if people knew.*

And what would Julian think? He'd come because he'd think he had to, because he was her employee, because he had to take pity on the old widow.

Still, every night the longing burned until it consumed all the other voices in her head, and she finally crossed the yard and asked him if he wouldn't have dinner with her every night.

She waited in trepidation, looking for the expression that would give away his reluctance. But the instant warmth in his voice surprised her.

"Are you sure, Leah? You don't have to do this."

She responded with hearty relief. "You're working all day in the cold, there's no way you can fix yourself enough to eat on that hot plate."

That was the end of it, and so their new routine began. Night after night when they came home, he'd shower and change into his one new flannel shirt before joining her in the kitchen.

She liked the way he'd ease into his chair, put his elbows on the table and inhale the cooking odors. At first, she'd insisted on doing the dishes, but one night, he planted himself at the sink and said, "No, you sit down." She watched as he rolled his sleeves up over his elbows. She turned on the radio and he sang along to *Honky Tonk Man*. His shoulders and hips swung as if he was about to launch onto a dance floor and whirl some skinny young thing around. She giggled and he looked over his shoulder and grinned at her.

At Christmas, she gave him two weeks off. On the morning he was to leave, she woke twitching in anticipation over the gift she had bought for him. How soon could she race to the bunkhouse and give it to him? She got up in the dark, paced for an hour, two hours, and when, at last, the hands on the rooster clock clicked to seven a.m., she snatched up the large package she'd wrapped the night before.

"Merry Christmas!" she crowed, but when she saw the open canvas bag on his bed, her enthusiasm faltered. It wasn't just that his departure was imminent. The bag hinted of a possibility she'd never thought of, the possibility that he might not return.

He was dressed to leave, in clean jeans and that one new flannel shirt he always wore to dinner.

"Leah…I didn't get you anything."

"You didn't have to. Go ahead. Open it."

"It's not Christmas."

"I want you to have it. Look, the card says, *Felice Navidad*."

"Spanish. That's very good, Leah."

He ripped the wrapping paper off in strips, opened the lid and lifted out a new Carhartt jacket. She waited for his face to light up, but the moments stretched awkwardly while he held up the coat and turned it around.

"I don't know what to say."

"Go ahead and try it on. It's just like Bud's."

"Yes, it's very big."

Maybe she had to explain it.

"That windbreaker that you wear...I don't know how you stay warm in that thing."

Julian stood slowly and put his arms in the sleeves. It was way too big. He looked down at where it hit midway down his thigh.

"I guess you're right about the size. I can exchange it."

He yanked it off, a little too quickly. "It's OK. Thank you for thinking of me."

"No, I'll do it. I want you to have it."

He folded it length-wise and laid it in her arms. How heavy it suddenly felt.

"You can come pick it up in a few days."

He shook his head. "I'll have it when I come back. After Christmas, I'm going to Albuquerque with my brothers for a few days."

"Albuquerque?" She glanced again at the open bag. "You hadn't told me that before."

He stared at her. "I didn't know that I needed to tell you everything. Leah, it's just a little trip. You don't have to worry. I'm coming back."

Leah couldn't suppress the stridency in her tone.

"Well, have a nice trip!" She wheeled and shut the door behind her.

The presumptions she'd made, how derelict they seemed. She'd come to think of him as a possession. The gift itself had just been another token of ownership. When, beyond the stout fences of the Bud Smalls ranch, events prowled that would pull him away, if not now, soon. *He will shed me just as he did this coat.*

The day after he left, she drove into Thistle for her Chuck-Wagon Gals meeting. Instead of a speaker, the program consisted of cooking awards for the Buckarettes, the group's junior organization. Tinsel streamers with sprigs of plastic holly crisscrossed the ceiling. Cowboy Santas, each with his own teeny-tiny lariat, festooned the tables. Leah ambled from one girl's crockpot to the next, pecking at the steaming contents. The Buckarettes drew smiles from the older women and they, in turn, tossed their permed tresses and giggled behind their serving tables, electrified by the attention. How lucky to wake each morning, perched at life's crest, surveying the candyland of possibility. Three years from now, she'd run into them at the dime store, in sweatpants with babies hanging off their arms.

She felt a hand on her arm and turned. It was Ginny.

"Leah, honey, I've just got to talk to you."

"Is there something wrong?"

Ginny manhandled her out of the line of traffic.

"I've heard some ugly talk. Lorena and Darcy—your sister-in-law—they say you're sleeping with that Mexican. I've stood up for you. I've said you're not like that. But you know how these things catch on."

Leah stared at the dyed honey-blond curls bobbing on top of Ginny's head, at her jowls, just starting to thicken. *Come to think of it, Ginny's put on quite a bit of weight since the last meeting.*

"How these things catch on..." Leah murmured, "I've been such a fool. I should have known from the moment Bud was wheeled out of the house...how these things catch on, how the cogs turn and suddenly, people you've known all your life turn against you."

"Honey, I don't know what you're talking about. I just don't want you to get hurt. If the Gals Board gets wind of it..."

"You believe it?"

Ginny squeezed Leah's hands. "I understand. You're lonely. I'd do it if...there was nothing else. The thing of it is, the Chuck-Wagon Gals just might let you go."

Leah peered back in the dining room at the kaleidoscope of women and girls milling round.

"Lives at the mercy of the Chuck-Wagon Gals. My, my, Ginny."

And back up the highway she went. Back under the *Bud Smalls Ranch* arch. Back to the snow-packed yard where her dog lay curled next to a planter of dead petunias. Back to the kitchen and rooster clock.

When Bud was alive, they'd traveled a hundred miles or more to the national forest to cut their Christmas tree every year, as well as trees for the brothers. In the first year or two of their marriage, she'd looked forward to the trip. The mountains glistened in the distance as they approached, the hot chocolate in the thermos always tasted so good, the silence of the forest was so deep and the pine scent, so pungent. But somewhere around trip number eight or nine, as she watched Bud check the tire chains, the anticipation of getting stuck in snow miles from the nearest telephone had lost its romantic allure. Still, they set off like mules in their traces. Last year they'd traveled there and back without one argument, actually without hardly any words between them at all.

This year she bought a fake tree, a troll-sized thing. She set it up in the living room next to Bud's recliner. The mountain pine scent was missing, but when the room was dark, the little colored lights blinked red and green, as they always had, little flares in the winter gloom.

Outside, no lights burned other than the yard light. The darkened bunkhouse drew her gaze—a black hole in space. How silly, all these years she'd never so much as glanced at that shack. A few short months with a light in the window had changed everything.

Leah pressed her forehead against the window and felt

the bitter cold seep through. She would go in the living room and turn up the TV to muffle the wind screeching about the house. After the news, she'd slip under her quilts and will herself to think of how she'd manage once Julian left for good. She wouldn't fall to pieces, she was past that now. She would write ads on little recipe cards and post them at the feed store. *Help Wanted*. The men who answered them, what would they look like? All she could picture were versions of Bud, who'd sooner or later, want to tell her what to do.

But she knew that when she drifted off to sleep, she'd see Julian dancing at the sink, that grin over his shoulder and the dimples at the corner of his mouth. The longing to mean more to him pierced her through, even as she chided herself for it. She would shut her eyes firmly, shove her head back in the pillow and resolve to be just another inert fixture in this house. *Until they hauled her carcass out of here.*

New Year's Day dawned like every other working day. No difference to it on a ranch. No floats of roses. The wind didn't take the day off to go muss up a parade or two. It rattled every loose scrap of tin roof, every gate hinge until the cacophony of banging, screeching, scratching, and rattling sounded like a New Year's band gone haywire. And she could hardly breathe from the hay whipping in her face as she tried to feed the horses.

Abruptly, she heard the puttering of a motor in the yard. Julian's motorcycle? Couldn't be, there was too much snow. She turned.

Sun glinted off a white Ski-doo, and the man riding it was Julian!

She dropped the pitchfork. She could hardly keep herself from running to him. It seemed to take an hour to cross the fifty yards between them.

"Where'd you come from? I thought you were in Albuquerque!"

He smiled. "Happy New Year's Day to you, too, Leah. I was there. I came back."

"On a Ski-doo?"

"I bought this before I left. It was broken. The guy who owned it, he didn't want to fix it, so I got to working on it a little. Now it runs good. This is your Christmas present, Leah."

Leah looked down at the sleek little nose of the machine and the gleaming edges of the runners. Her emotions spun around in her head like pinballs. Julian had gotten her a gift. *A gift he'd worked on. But a Ski-doo?* Bud had always hooted the word with contempt. "Gizmos for rich city fellers who think this country is some kinda Disneyland."

"Julian, what am I going to do with that?"

"Next time you get snowed in, Leah, you don't have to wait for someone to clear roads for you. You don't have to depend on anyone, anymore. You can take the snowmobile to town. You can get groceries. You can have coffee with the Cattle Ladies."

"I'm not driving that thing."

"You have so much happening today you cannot try it?"

She was so happy to see him that she would have tried to stand on her head if he asked.

"OK. I'll try it."

She straddled the seat. Merle and Grady would be slapping one another if they were zooming their lenses in on her now. When Julian plopped in front of her, her heart jolted at how close he was. In her rush to scoot back, she nearly fell off the back end.

Julian shifted to look back at her. "You all right?"

"There's not enough room on this thing!"

He shot off and the sagebrush turned into a pea-soup smear as they whooshed by. An eagle flew up as they approached, startled off a jackrabbit kill. Julian accelerated

212

and they climbed the butte overlooking her buildings, her meadows, her cattle.

He cut the engine. Below, cows drifted to the haystack, patiently waiting for the tractor to come spread their hay. The stacks of bales she and Julian had put up over the summer were mounded with snow. Beyond the pastures squared by fence lines, snowdrifts undulated on to the horizon. Sunlight streamed down on a world glittering white.

A paradise. If an afterlife existed, could it overcome one's heart, as this world did? Julian stood next to her, also gazing out over the countryside. Did he feel it as she did? She didn't know how to ask him, and he offered nothing. Maybe he'd become indifferent. Or like Bud, maybe he'd never noticed at all. Yet he had brought her here.

A shadow grazed her field of vision and she glanced up to watch the eagle, spiraling ever higher.

The snow crunched beneath them as Julian shifted to face her.

"Now, are you ready to learn?"

And if Grady and Merle were watching, they'd have seen her buzzing over the range with her Mexican behind her.

In her dream her Ski-doo fell out from under her and a jet stream, like the one on the weatherman's maps, whooshed her along through space. Images from her life shot by like billboards. At intervals, she heard a pounding. She tried to focus on it, but each time it stopped, she surrendered back into the current. Her hand flailed. She expected it to land on a man's bulk beside her. When it flopped against the sheet, she woke.

The glow of a full moon shone through her curtain. The pounding on the door...Julian.

She threw on her robe and ran barefooted across the cold linoleum floor. In the porch light, Julian was fully dressed for work in his lined cap, coveralls and mittens. And his new proper sized Carhartt jacket.

"It's time, Leah."

"A heifer in labor?"

"Yes."

In January, when they'd discussed calving, Julian had told her she had to learn to deliver calves. She had immediately blurted, "I can't." In the pause that followed, Julian leaned over the table. Without a trace of rancor or sarcasm, he'd said, "You have two hundred and thirty-five mama cows. Thirty first-time mamas-to-be. And all must be fed every day. We can't always work together, and if you are here by yourself, you must know how to do this if all the calves are to survive."

OK. So her first calf had to come in the dead of night.

"Let me get dressed."

The phone rang. Both of them stared at it, startled. It rang twice more before Leah picked it up, listened and held it out to Julian.

He answered in Spanish, but she didn't need a translator to know what was being said. The tones were all too familiar. In the pause that followed once the receiver clicked into place, she knew that everything had shifted between them.

"My mother is dying."

"You need to go."

"First, we will pull your calf."

"Leave it. Go."

"My brother is coming to get me. It will take them a little while to get here."

She expected him to look anxious, but no such emotion broke in his features. The news hadn't yet settled, she decided. It was easier for him to grasp this urgency than the other one where no amount of his know-how would apply.

She thought she'd dressed warmly enough, but once they plunged into the deep night, the cold slashed through every layer she wore. She huffed behind him to the calving shed. He had already secured the heifer and underneath the fluorescent light, she stood in the stanchion, trembling.

"Why is she shaking like that?" asked Leah.

"She is in pain. Shock. She is afraid."

"She'd be terrified if she knew I was the one helping her."

"That's very funny, Leah. But in a few moments, you will do this as well as if you had done it a hundred times."

Julian showed her how to assemble the calf-puller, slide her hands into the heifer's vulva and wrap bracelet chains around the calf's feet. Leah waited for the contractions before she began to pull. As cold as she'd been moments before, she was sweating as if she herself was in labor. *Gimme that,* that's what Bud would be saying now. Instead, Julian leaned against the rail, softly murmuring instructions.

As the calf's nose and head emerged, Leah forgot her revulsion at the blood and slime and manure. The creature was encased in its delicate wrap, like a gift. Contraction by contraction, her own pulse quickened with this new life she was coaxing into existence until, with a wet plop, the calf landed at her feet. Only then did Julian leap in the pen and remove the sack from its head. The calf sputtered, coughed, breathed. Life, like the flick of a match into flame.

Julian released the heifer from the stanchion and hustled Leah out of the pen.

"They need time alone."

She looked back over her shoulder at the heifer nosing her wriggling baby.

Outside the shed door, they blinked in the headlights of a vehicle waiting in the yard. The lights and the rumbling motor struck her as a profanity after the miracle they'd just witnessed. Behind the vehicle, a band of sky blanched above the horizon.

"Will you be all right?" Julian asked.

From the day he'd first rode up on his motorcycle, he'd worn a young man's self-assurance as easily as his own skin. Now, she saw fissures of doubt and fear in his eyes that had never been there before. He wasn't sure that he would be all right. Maybe she had a skill to show him after all. Although she hadn't known how to put up hay, manhandle barbed wire, drive Ski-doos or birth calves, she knew how to negotiate the span over loss.

She squeezed his arm.

"I'll be all right, Julian. You take your time."

He reached up and pushed back her hood. Then he put his arm around her and kissed her on the forehead, just at the place where her scalp was balding.

The idea that she had something to give back, in return for the work that had saved her, lingered in her mind through the funeral at the little Catholic church, through the procession up the goat path to Thistle's cemetery where the edges of the canopy whipped in the wind and the Hanson boy, with his hands folded, tried to suppress his shivering. It stayed with her through the dinners when Julian said nothing at all and on through each night as they took turns checking heifers under stars so thick they seemed to spill into the yard, or in blizzards that piled drifts so deep they'd spend hours plowing come the next morning.

And then one dawn found them in her kitchen after they'd been up all night birthing calves. Julian was washing out his coffee cup at the sink.

His shoulders slumped, but he said, "I know you are tired, Leah. Go lie down and I will feed."

He didn't turn. He put down the dishrag and remained there, staring out the window as little by little, the sun arced over the miles of range that ran beyond what the eye could take in, beyond what the heart could grasp.

She sidled up to him and laid her head against his shoulder. He shifted slightly, his chin rubbing that same spot on her forehead that he had kissed. Then he rested his head down on hers. She felt the scratchiness of his stubble and the rustle of his shirt as he breathed. Under her breath, she started to sing

I Can't Help It If I'm Still in Love With You. He laughed a little, then sang the chorus with her. They put their arms around each other and swayed for a while at the sink until they turned, encircled one another and shuffled a two-step over the scuffed linoleum.

VII

Memorial Day and still little caps of dirt-caked snow clung to the graves in Thistle's cemetery. A tart breeze rattled the sagebrush, and Leah was glad she'd worn Bud's coat. Through her knee-pads, heat from the ground radiated up her thighs, and she felt comfortable enough to break off spading dirt and watch a coyote weave among the plots. He caught her odor, stopped, and they regarded each other. By the way he sniffed the wind, Leah could tell he wasn't frightened, just puzzled at why she lingered when all the other humans trooped here in noisy herds and departed. No matter. He turned and trotted on.

The plastic flowers left on graves looked more like trash than memorials, especially against the soft pastels of the greening prairie. One glance at the place a few weeks ago had convinced Leah that the only fitting memorial was a living one, and for Bud, what better than flowering cactus?

Within the shelter of the rocks that Julian had hauled, she transplanted cactus from the ranch. Buds already swelled on the plants, and with any luck, after those plastic flowers were covered in dirt, the lemon yellow of her flowers would draw bees, hummingbirds, and hearts longing for comfort.

At the crest of the hill, she paused and watched Thistle below her, as she had a year ago. The same old stoplight turned red, green, and then yellow, the same tourists with the same children on their way to Yellowstone paused there, briefly relieved by the sight of something other than empty range. The same old pageant grinding by.

Funny. Merle's emerald Lincoln was parked next to her pickup, and the Smalls brothers stood there ogling her. *Déjà vu*, except she wasn't tripping down the hill wearing her *Gabriella* perfume. This time she wore work boots.

As she approached, she was surprised to see that the men no longer matched up with the images she'd retained of them. Merle's belly had expanded over his belt and his shoulders seemed to have sunk, probably dragged down by the weight of that gut. Grady's neck was scrawny as a turkey's and his mustache had turned white. Both mens' chests looked deflated.

If they were surprised to see her dressed like Bud, they didn't react.

Merle tipped his hat. "'Morning, Leah."

She looked from brother to brother. Surely, they hadn't shown up to share old times. Her heart skipped a moment— they were here to confront her over Julian. She should've expected it before now, really. The intimations among the Chuck-Wagon Gals last Christmas would have gathered mass over the winter. Especially when she'd never returned to refute them.

Grady spoke. "We looked for you at the place. Julian said you were here."

Then Merle. "How about some coffee in town?"

"I haven't got the time for it now," she said.

They looked stunned, as if she'd wounded them.

"We want to talk to ya," said Grady, "We haven't visited in a long time."

"I'm standing right here."

The brothers looked at one another. Those two couldn't unzip their flies without checking with one another. Grady cleared his throat.

"We want to talk to ya about the offer for the place.

We've been thinking…it was too low. We've come up with a new figure." He handed her a sheet of paper.

She looked down and studied it.

"Well," said Merle, "what do you say?"

"I don't understand this."

"It's about keeping the place in the family. That's what we want. That's what Bud would have wanted. You know what it meant to him. And he would have wanted you to be taken care of."

Leah smiled. "Has he been haunting you two?"

They looked at one another again.

Grady blurted, "It's just that…have you thought about what happens when you pass on? You know who that ranch belongs to, who has a history there. Not that we got a thing against Mexicans, but after you're gone, we don't want to be haggling over water rights with, well, strangers."

Merle picked up the thread, spun it out. "Look, Leah, we don't care who you sleep with. There's people that do, but we don't. We don't judge you. We just want you to think on all the years we've been family. A long time, Leah. A lot of water under the bridge." He nodded toward the piece of paper. "We're thinking with that increase in price, we'll all get what we want."

She smiled as she put it in her pocket. "And I can go to Arizona?"

"With that wad, Paris, France, if you want to," said Grady.

"With me gone, what would you boys do in your spare time?" They both stared at her, straight-faced. Funny how the "boys" had turned into two old men.

"If you'll excuse me, I've got some irrigating to do at home."

"Don't you want to talk about it?" Merle called after her.

In her rearview mirror, she saw them rooted behind the emerald Lincoln, diminishing to pygmies as she accelerated.

All the way home Leah smiled thinking of how she'd share the story with Julian. He'd grin as she crowed over how she'd ditched them in the parking lot.

She found him replacing a rotten post in the corrals. His cap was pushed back on his head, and his tattered shirttails hung over his jeans. The coat she'd given him lay on the ground. *Dammit, wouldn't he think to take better care of it than that? Nevermind.*

"Julian, you'll never guess who I saw at the cemetery."

The story gushed out of her mouth, but Julian only grunted as he tamped dirt around the post. She finished by whipping the paper from her pocket.

"And look! Look how much they're offering for the place now. Twice as much as last year, the sonsofbitches!"

She paused, waiting for his encouragement. Instead, he tested his post and hoisted the tamping bar again without so much as a glance at her piece of paper.

She picked the coat off the ground and threw it over the rail. "Am I missing something? Is something the matter?"

He rested the tamping bar against the new post and turned to her.

"I've talked to my cousin, Ricky. He can help you hay this summer. The fences are all fixed and the water is running on the meadows."

"What are you talking about?"

He ran his thumbnail up and down the post, flicking off the splinters.

"I am grateful to you, Leah. You were very good to me after my mother died. I'll never forget it. You worked so hard outside with me, and then you came in and fixed dinners and I said nothing. The days went by, and all I could think about was how mad I was that my time with her was all used up, that there wasn't one more hour left. Every day you live and live and then it's just over, just like that, like none of it ever even mattered.

"And then that morning you sang Hank Williams." He shrugged, "It was just a little thing, but it felt like...somebody's throwing me a lifeline. Do you understand that?"

"I understand."

"I don't want you to think...that I don't care."

"So what are you saying?"

"I am going to leave."

"Grady and Merle, those two said something to you, didn't they?"

He shook his head. "They didn't say nothin'. It's been a year since I came and...I have to think, Leah. I mean, I got nothing here."

"You're a part of my life and that's nothing?"

"I'm not part of your life. You are the Widow Smalls. That house over there, you live in it with Mr. Smalls. I always feel like he is still there. Even when we started sleeping together, I felt like I'm just the hired man."

She gasped. "You've never complained before now. And you certainly never acted as if our bed was a chore. And why? I'll tell you why — so you could come and go just as you wanted! Like maybe take a trip to Albuquerque!"

He put his hands on his hips. "OK, Leah. So you would marry me if I asked. You would share this ranch with me."

Take him into Bud's house? As her husband? She fumbled for plausible excuses.

"It's ridiculous. I'm old. I couldn't have children for you. I thought you were comfortable, that you had everything you wanted."

"There is nothing more I can help you with here. Go back to your house, Ms. Smalls. And decide. Whether you are going to be the Widow Smalls. Or whether you will have a life. Any life. The ranch does not care who claims it."

He strode away from her. The tamping bar slipped off the post and fell with a clang. What could she say to make him turn around? There was nothing to say.

She went back to her kitchen, unfolded the paper Grady had given her and smoothed it out on the table.

VII

"The damn woman's witless," said Merle as he slathered his steak with A-1 Sauce.

The other men at the table, members of Thistle's livestock association, nodded in sympathy.

"She was always odd. Darcy'll tell ya. Never mingled with the family. You'd have thought that without children, she'd have been out there helping Bud." He shook his head. "She never did. Heck, the lack of help prob'ly killed him.

"We offered her a bundle for that ranch. Well, it's our ranch, really. Our daddy's. You can't say she cared about it when she never so much as stuck her nose out the door. She hemmed and hawed around, finally told us she was willin' to part with some summer pasture. We took that, figuring it'd be just a matter of time before she let the rest go. Her Mexican left, so we didn't think she could hang on for long.

"But damn. In the fall, Grady and I were out at the fence line. We weren't spying on her. We were out looking for trespassin' hunters. Grady got out his binoculars and damn if the house wasn't being torn down!

"So Darcy sent out some of the Chuck-Wagon Gals to see if she'd gone stark mad, and they come back, said she'd decided the house wasn't good enough no more. She was gonna live in the bunkhouse, redo it as a kind of cabin, or some other foolishness.

"Bud never oughtta've married her. We warned him the day of the wedding. And now here we are. With a witless hen right smack in our backyard. And we can't get rid of her."

Merle and Grady had only seen part of the demolition, not all of it. For the last segment, she hired the very same Hanson boy who'd buried Bud.

As Leah and Pepper waited under the rusted arch, they watched the boy rattle up the road in a giant bulldozer. It seemed to take him forever to get there.

He didn't want to talk much. He said they needed to get on with it, he had a funeral at two.

The machine clanked and screeched and groaned as he raised the bucket high up over the arch. He shinnied up it and ran a chain between the words "Bud" and "Smalls." He waved Leah and Pepper out of the way and once they'd reached a respectable distance, the bulldozer slowly reversed, the arch creaked, then snapped at the base and crashed down.

Leah took a Polaroid snapshot of the Hanson boy and Pepper standing on the downed arch. She scratched a few words on a note, slipped it in an envelope with the picture and handed it to the mail lady when she drove past.

Julian came into the post office at Dubois. The rest of the fencing crew invited him for a beer. Just give him a minute, he'd said, to check his mail. He opened his box, saw the envelope and opened it, looked at the picture.

The handwritten note read, "The Ruiz place?"

Julian had a pickup now, fire-engine red, that he'd salvaged from a junkyard. He stopped at the last gas station out of Dubois. And then down the road he floored it, eighty-five miles an hour, fast as that truck would go, toward Thistle, toward a woman who was done being the Widow Smalls.

Jamie Lisa Forbes

Acknowledgments

Much thanks to Susan Eastman and Annette Chaudet for criticism and encouragement.

Thank you to Lauren Sarraf for all your assistance, advice, encouragement and advocacy. You are the best daughter in the world.

Thank you to Vance Barron, Jr. for all your work on the author photograph.

Thank you to Trish Nelson and Letty Coykendall for assistance with the final editing.

Thank you to Leonard Johnson who always had time for one more story.

Thank you to Joe Coykendall who taught me the value of listening. May their memories be for a blessing.

Jamie Lisa Forbes

About the Author

Jamie Lisa Forbes was raised on a family ranch in southeastern Wyoming. She graduated from the University of Colorado with honors in 1977 and then lived in Israel until 1979, when she returned to her family's ranch and raised her own family over the next fifteen years. Today, she writes and practices law in Greensboro, North Carolina. She enjoys spending time with her grandsons and playing old time Appalachian fiddle. With her Arabian horse, Cody, and her cattle dog, Reb, she still devotes part of her life to the outdoors.

Jamie Lisa Forbes

The Widow Smalls and Other Stories